# Up All Night

## A True (Enough) Story

**Cynthia Dane**
BARACHOU PRESS

**Up All Night**

Copyright: Cynthia Dane
Published: 2nd February 2017
Publisher: Barachou Press

\* \* \*　一期一会　\* \* \*

## A Word From Your Narrator

The story you're about to read is true.

Mostly.

As with any supposedly true story, there are things that must be altered or outright changed in order to create a fulfilling reading experience. If I told you exactly how this story happened, you'd be disappointed with the ending, and we cannot have that. What we must have, however, is a fun, sexy, and even uplifting experience – the reading experience you came to me for.

So this is a true story. The setting, the setup, the thoughts and feelings permeating the scenes, many of the scenes themselves... shit, some of the background characters are 100% authentic, although names and some descriptions have been changed to protect the poor fools. I strove for as much authenticity as possible. The story could have only happened in Japan, for example. Plus, I'm not going to pretend I'm some eyelash-batting virgin who doesn't know what a one-night-stand that turns into something more feels like. I've been writing naughty romance stories for yonks. Those stories have origins in my own life, don't they?

But this is the first time I've decided to write a story that is lifted directly from my own personal experiences. Once the events unfolded, I couldn't help but laugh at what a perfectly good romantic comedy they would make. So here we are, in the year of our Lord 2017, talking about an event that befell yours truly in November, 2016. Some of you were even there for it if you followed my erratic Facebook posts.

Yet there is a huge drawback to being so open with my personal experiences. The great thing about fiction is that it builds a natural wall between the characters and reader. That wall says, "You can peer into these people's sex lives because they're not actually real." When that wall comes down, things get awkward, don't they?

So here is what I propose: we treat the following story as another fictional account that sprang from my head like Athena from Zeus, and we keep it at that. Cyndi is me, but she's not *really* me. Her hunky date says and does many things the date of infamy said, but in reality, he's a composite of many men Cyndi has met in her life. And the ending? Pure tosh, but it's happy tosh that creates the story we truly want to tell and read.

I'm open with you about the ending, but how could everything else be true?

It's true because you trust me to tell you it's true – and mean it.

# Up All Night

Anything you read that makes you go, "Would a guy actually say that?" or, "Oh my God, I've totally had that happen to me!" means that, yes, it happened. My hand on my heart and swearing to that same God we were talking about.

Imagine us as best friends, Reader. Imagine us in a coffee shop, where the music is loud enough to keep eavesdroppers from overhearing our sordid tales of men past. Imagine me drinking tea and you drinking your favorite beverage that you've decided to treat yourself to, because this is Girl's Day, and we are having a grand time talking about our current partners and the men and women who made up our pasts. Without those people, we wouldn't be who we are today, and that's my intention with telling you about what happened to me in November, 2016.

That and a lot of it was really fucking funny. I mean, really, a neighbor who times himself having sex and a date who spends half the night apologizing for his dick? That shit's hilarious, and I need to gab about it.

Join me in my tale of frustration, sleep anxiety, the craziest ovulation cycle a woman has ever gone through, and the one night that made it all worthwhile. I've even Romanced the ending for you in case you love your happy endings as much as I do. (Besides, I said that Cyndi isn't *me* me! That girl needs a happy ending!)

I'll let you get up and retrieve your drink, though. You might also want to make sure you go to the bathroom first. We're gonna be here a while, and you'll be laughing.

Let me start by saying I was in Tokyo for a workcation…

\* \* \* 一期一会 \* \* \*

## Chapter 1

I hadn't slept in three fucking days.

My neighbor. It was my stupid neighbor whose name I could not tell you now. All I knew was that he was French (because everyone in my share house was French,) and had recently quit his job to, I don't know, lift weights at the gym all day and make food in the kitchen that I always had to clean up.

Basically, this guy was annoying enough when he *wasn't* keeping me awake 24/7.

You tell someone, "My French neighbor kept me up for three days straight," and the first thing they do is nudge you with a wink and reply, "That good, huh?" Honey, I wish this guy was boning me for three days straight. I *wish* I was the one he was fucking, because then at least I was getting some.

No. He was fucking his girlfriend. All day. All night.

You ever stay in a share house? It's the only way to stay in Tokyo for a month or two, in my humble opinion. You can rent a private room in a share house for a month and spend *less* than a hotel room for half that time. So, if you're paying a grand on plane tickets, you might as well spring for a month-long trip and make the best of your stay. This was actually my second time, although the first time in this share house.

Japanese houses have the thinnest walls. They must be the origin of *paper thin walls,* and that paper is made out of rice. Even so, you know that going into a share house situation. You know that you'll hear them snoring, and that they'll hear you when you catch the cough everyone on the subway had. It's a part of life. But unlike a college dorm situation, the people in a share house tend to skew older and more mature.

You hope, anyway.

Hearing my neighbor have sex was not unexpected. Like I said, these people were adults and had adult lives. Sometimes it can't be helped – you've gotta go back to your crappy dorm room to get off with your girl. (Never mind we were in the country full of love hotels, but I'll get to that later.) Damn be your neighbors.

Damn be me, because this wasn't a one-time thing to giggle over. This was every two hours for three days straight.

Think I'm kidding? I'm not. My neighbor and his girlfriend were sex machines. From the moment I walked into my room after a day of doing touristy stuff, I was treated to the grunts, groans, and *wails* of two twenty-somethings rutting like animals. Before I came to Japan, I had no idea how to talk dirty in French. After I left Japan, I knew how to make a girl come – but don't quote me on my accent.

Cynthia Dane

Here's the crazy thing that led to everyone in the share house thinking they (or the guy, at least) had some serious addiction. They'd fuck, get off, roll over and fall asleep – I know, because he snored – and then two hours later their alarms went off and they fucked again.

I'm not kidding. They woke themselves up every two hours to have sex. For 12-15 hours straight.

I can't make this shit up. When I realized what was going on, I wanted to scream at them. How fucking dare they! Some of us were trying to *sleep*, for God's sake. My natural sleep rhythm puts me between four in the morning and noon. These two were going at it until late in the morning. Do you know what having to constantly listen to two people have sex is like? When you're trying to sleep?

Let me guess what you're thinking right now. *"What about eeaaar pluuuuugs, Cynnnndiiii."* Bugger off. Ear plugs don't do shit, are you kidding me? I bought two pairs and neither one of them even dulled the moaning and bed creaking! Not even a little bit! My next grab for peace was installing a white noise app on my phone and plugging in my (uncomfortable) headphones, but the internet was so spotty (and obviously I did not have data in a foreign country) that it didn't work most of the time.

Besides, the problem wasn't the actual sex noises as much as it was that damned piece of shit bed hitting my wall every two seconds.

*Bang! Bang! Bang!* Grunt, growl, ejaculate. Snore. Rinse and repeat two hours later.

# Up All Night

That bed banging made my room shake more than the two earthquakes I tried to sleep through while I was there. Shit fell off my desk. The clock on the wall rattled. I'm pretty sure dust fell from the ceiling. (Speaking of my upstairs neighbor, the only thing I ever heard was the occasional flushing of the toilet right above my head.) No matter what I did, going deaf would not have stopped those idiots next door from keeping me awake for three days in a row.

By that third night, friends, I had serious sleep anxiety. Which is sad, because occasionally they took a four hour (four whole hours!) break that I could've gotten some serious sleep in, but by that time my brain was wired to expect the worst every time I closed my eyes. *"What's the point, Cyndi? They're going to wake you up again. You're not going to sleep again, and tomorrow you'll be so tired and dead at work that you'll be crying in a Japanese Starbucks. Again."*

So when they started having sex at 5am, I lost my cool.

"Shut the fuck up!" I shouted through the wall. I leaped out of the bed and took the one step necessary to our shared wall. After I gave it a hearty pounding (har, har,) I yelled at them to please, please stop having sex because some of us really wanted to sleep!

Trust me, by that point I had lost my mind to fatigue and had no sense of shame. Clearly, these people had no shame either. I've heard some stereotypical stuff about the French before, but this took the cake.

Suffice to say, those assholes did not give up their fornicating reign.

What does a girl do when she hasn't slept in three days because her neighbors are horny assholes? Why, she goes to her Facebook and rants about it to anyone who will listen.

*"Please save me, I haven't slept in three days. Neighbors are still having sex."*

Most people feel for you. Others try to be slick and suggest that they're stamina training or going for a baby. Because that totally makes it okay!

Then you get those who are convinced this guy must have his girlfriend tied up in his room and is using her as a sex slave. (Why am I not calling the police, though?) Or that the girlfriend doesn't actually exist and we are witnessing one French man's descent into sexual madness. (That's some serious arthouse, though.) Me? I didn't care if this guy was jacking off to porn. (And he did. Often. I could give you details about that too.) I cared that he was forcing me to be an unwilling audience to his sex life and keeping me from a basic bodily function while his went into overdrive.

I felt powerless. And full of petty revenge. When those two things collide, you make some interesting life choices.

**\*\*\***

"What do you think about your neighbor?"

I lifted my head off the couch while some Japanese news report played on the TV. For the past few days the news had not let up on this huge marijuana bust that went down somewhere. As an Oregonian, I often forgot that there were places in the world where smoking pot was a huge deal. I'm used to smelling it wherever I go. (In Japan, you smell regular ol' tobacco wherever you go. Fuck it.)

The woman talking to me was a Turkish resident who had been friendly since the first day I moved in. I couldn't tell you her name like I couldn't tell you the name of my irritating neighbor. When you're only staying for a month, it's difficult to remember the unfamiliar names of people you're only going to see once or twice in your life.

"I hate him." I almost knocked my lunch plate off my lap. "I haven't slept in three fucking days because of him."

"Oh my *God*, me too!" She spun around from the gas stove. The November cold had fogged up the window, and yet for some reason the damn thing was open wide and letting in every freezing breeze. "Do you hear it every night?"

"Yes! They have so much sex I can't sleep!"

"Same!" She rushed over to me. "I thought maybe I was making things up at first. But, you know, it's not the first time something like this has happened. Before you moved here, it happened sometimes. Recently it's been the worse ever."

"Do you hear them set the alarm so they can have sex?"

"Oh my God! So you hear it too?"

"Do you ever actually see his girlfriend? I don't hear her get up to use the bathroom afterward." I'm not kidding, folks. Not once, in the midst of all this fucking, did she use the bathroom. The UTI was going to be unreal.

"I saw her one time. She ran back into his room so fast I barely realized it was her."

"Oh, good, I was starting to wonder if she actually existed."

"Yeah, she's Japanese."

The only reason that was surprising – we were in Japan, after all – was because he had spoken so much damn French while fucking her that I assumed it was a Frenchwoman on the other end of his relentless dick.

"Have you said anything to him?" I asked.

My new friend scoffed. "Are you kidding? I try to say something like I am trying to sleep... but they keep going. Bang, bang, bang."

"Right? It's the bed that kills you."

"The stupid bed always hitting the... oh my God, you have it worse! I know the layout of his room, and his bed is right up against your wall. You poor thing."

Poor thing was right. Woe was me. The girl who couldn't escape that fucking bullshit.

"Know what I wanna do?" I hauled my ass to the sink and rinsed off my plate. "I wanna find some jerk to bring in there and give that guy a taste of his own medicine."

"Hell yes! I haven't been in a relationship in a long time, so I can't really have fantasies about that... but if you can, bring your boyfriend over and fuck him really loud. We'll all ignore it for a night if it means that asshole knows what it's like to lose sleep over someone's sex life."

"Too bad I don't have one. A boyfriend, that is."

She crossed her arms. "You could get one. Men are easy in Tokyo."

Yeah, I'd heard that before.

* * *   一期一会   * * *
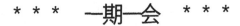

# Chapter 2

One thing that I didn't want to admit to anyone was that, even with my lack of sleep and general disdain for the world, I was going through one of the wildest ovulations of my life.

How the hell else do I describe it? It was going on before my neighbor started acting up, and no, listening to his fuckfests did *not* make me hornier. If anything, that man was doing everything in his libidic power to kill any interest I would have in sex again.

Then I lived my day to day life.

Have you ever been so damn *horny* that your whole body is constantly shaking with thoughts of getting laid? I'm not kidding. Whenever I had actual moments to myself that weren't fueled by my hatred for my neighbor, I ended up in a dark hellscape where I was not getting any.

It did not help that I worked during my supposed vacation. As a romance author, I spend a lot of my time writing about other people having sex. Usually this isn't a big deal. Honestly, half the time I groan to think I have to write *more sex* even though it's the farthest thing from my own mind. Yet as I sat in my local Starbucks, overlooking a major Tokyo intersection, with my screen open to some sizzling sex between a billionaire and his curvy little sweetie, I thought, *"Fuck it! I want some too!"*

I'm not going to get into the details of my love life leading up to this trip. All you need to know is two things: I wasn't a virgin, and I really, really craved some masculine company.

Okay, so I lied. Here's a piece of pie for your sweet tooth.

It had been years – actual, literal *years* – since I was last with a man. I think my body had been reminded of that fact to the point it would not let it fucking go. I was going to watch every paired off couple sneak into a love hotel with as much jealousy as I could harbor in my poor, shaking body.

Every inch of my skin was alive with nobody to touch it.

Every dirty thought that entered my mind was practically broadcasted to the crowded room.

Every decent-looking man who came within my vicinity was automatically the subject of five-thousand fantasies. Sometimes I entertained the idea that I was a part of their fantasies too.

I endured this horrible state for days. Luckily, when you're self-employed *and* traveling around a foreign country, you have plenty to distract yourself with. You've got that crippling sense of dread that you're an abject failure if you're not actively working on a project even at one in the morning. (Assuming your music is loud enough to drown out the fucking going on next door.) You can also go shopping and amuse yourself with a boatload of new CDs (shut up) and office supplies, because Japan does CD shopping and office supplies the *best*.

Yet nothing can save you from yourself once you actually do have a few minutes of peace in your mind. In your room. In your bed.

So I couldn't sleep thanks to the anxiety my wonderful neighbor gave me. I also couldn't sleep because my body was about to burst if I didn't get some soon. Basically, my existence was consumed with sex, and it wasn't pretty.

For some reason, Starbucks is so much more expensive in Japan than it is in America. Fun fact: I never stepped into a Starbucks until I lived in Japan years ago. Another fun fact: most of my novels are written in a Starbucks near you. So even though a Grande English Breakfast tea costs a dollar more in Japan than it does in America, and a chocolate chip scone likewise costs my non-existent first born, my work brain associates Starbucks with getting shit done.

Picture me, at this upscale Starbucks in the Iidabashi neighborhood, where traditional Edo meets modern Tokyo, sitting at a crowded counter with barely enough room for my netbook and my tray of goodies. On one side of me is a geologist studying charts and graphs on his computer that looks like it's stuck in 2005. On the other side of is a young, fashionable student more interested in her makeup than the biology materials in her textbook. I chugged that English Breakfast with gusto, because I was so fucking tired that the words did not appear in my word processor.

*"Bring your boyfriend over and fuck him really loud."*

I opened up Facebook and read the latest comments on my debacle of a post. *"Suppose they're not French enough to invite you for a ménage, huh?"*

A part of me wanted to go home and rest, but I knew that there was no rest as long as my neighbor's libido remained unsated. Like mine.

That dude needed to be put into his place. *I* needed to get laid. Surely, there was some way I could make these two things happen. Perhaps simultaneously.

**\*\*\***

I had reached a new low.

Never before had a dating app graced my phone. Never before had I connected my Facebook (my work Facebook! What the fuck was I thinking? God! It said CYNDI under a picture of me. What was I? Some stripper?) to an app used to get honeys. Male honeys. Male honeys that had either lived in Japan for so long that they were jaded fucks, or were passing through and on a hunt for Japanese pussy to satisfy their life-long fetishes. (So, you know, neither gave a fuck about me.)

*I can't believe I'm doing this,* I thought as I sprawled across my bed and hastily created a profile. I kept telling myself that this was a game, a lark, something I never had to go through with if I felt uncomfortable later on. Yes, yes, placate myself with promises that I could ghost any dude, or that I could nuke this app from orbit once I came to my senses.

Although, if you've ever been as hard up for a date as I was, you know that there is no coming to one's senses until it's too late.

I took a few cute selfies and uploaded them. I explained in my profile that I was only in town for a couple more weeks, so I wasn't looking for anything serious outside of a few dates. (Guys were into that, right? You always heard from women on dating sites that guys wanted to hook up. Well, I wanted to hook up! That should land me *lots* of hot dudes, right? Good looking ones? Decent looking ones? Ones I could sleep with while the lights were off?) The only thing I said about myself was that my name wasn't actually Cyndi in real life, regardless of what my profile forced me to say. I had a feeling most guys wouldn't care. If anything, they probably felt sorry for me because my name was *Cyndi*.

I popped open a bag of chocolate-covered peanuts before activating my profile. If I were the drinking type, I would've had a beer or a glass of wine to lubricate this bullshit.

Right away the app prompted me to start swiping right or left on the faces of men from all over the world.

It's dirty business choosing who you date in this fashion. It feels even less nice when you realize that men are doing the same thing to you. Some guy was sitting on the Tokyo Metro swiping through pictures of women while his dick twitched and thirsted for some pussy. He lingered on my photo and either shrugged before swiping right, or immediately swiped left because he thought I was ugly. (Or because I wasn't Japanese. Extra nice.)

- 15 -

I had to be mercenary. I wasn't going to settle. If I sank to this low, then I needed to be as critical – or not as critical – as the men judging me based off one photo.

Don't ask me what my type is when it comes to the male half of the species. Do you look like a serial killer? Goodbye. Do you have a beard that looks like it wants to slice me in half? *Bye.* Does the only picture you provide give me hints that hygiene is secondary to your life? Haha. No.

Don't even have a picture of yourself? Nope. Open your profile with *"No fatties thanks,"* then wow, how do I have this sinking feeling that you think I'm too fat in my size 10 jeans? Do your photos show a woman and children that suspiciously look like they're related to you?

(Do I have to go on?)

I had never done something like that before, yet it was unnerving how quickly I acclimated to judging men based solely on their appearance and whether or not a cursory glance at their short profile made them sound like sociopaths. Honestly, I didn't care if they were in relationships or not. (As long as they didn't bring them up, I suppose.) This was about a one night fling, a quick jab at some hot sex, assuming the universe had that much pleasure in store for me.

Noses squished beneath my thumb. Receding hairlines pressed against my index finger. Goofy smiles and bulging muscles I knew I were never going to touch (because guys that hot don't settle for girls not as hot as *them*) flew by so quickly that I couldn't tell you if I hated them or…

*"Congrats! It's a match!"*

## Up All Night

Wait, who was this guy? Oh, no. Oh no. I had accidentally swiped right on a guy with an actual neckbeard and opened his profile with, *"I don't want a woman who is full of herself and wants me to take care of her. If you're someone who doesn't fall for beauty standards, then I would love to go dutch on some coffee with you."*

How did I even…

*"Hi,"* the dude *immediately* messaged me, *"you seem like a smart young woman from your profile. Care to have coffee with me?"*

I had never blocked a man so quickly. Nor had I ever tossed my phone across my bed and buried myself beneath a pile of blankets, but hey, there is a first time for everything, right?

God, this had clearly been a mistake. After sleeping on it, I decided pto completely deactivate the whole thing and go back to my miserable existence as the horniest woman in Tokyo who never got any sleep because everyone else had more sex than her.

Then I woke up.

* * *  一期一会 * * *

# Chapter 3

"*Hi.*"

I rubbed my eyes as I rolled over, seemingly awake. Hard to tell back then since I was going on my fourth day of *meh* sleep. While my neighbor had toned it down a bit, my brain was still doing that thing where it didn't want to let me sleep. And once I did, the rest of the household woke up to get ready for work and college classes, and guess what my other wall bordered? The kitchen.

Two messages from two different men greeted me. The aforementioned salutation, and another one. A much longer one.

"*Hello! I have to say you are a beautiful specimen of the Japanese race...*"

Because nothing said "Good morning, Cyndi!" like being the target of some white guy's misdirected Asian fetishism. Next.

# Up All Night

Mr. *Hi.*

That's all he said. No introduction, no asking how I was, how I liked Japan... a simple hello, accompanied with a shot of the right side of his face and the name *Hadrian*. I had never heard of it before.

His profile wasn't much help either. A lot of emoticons and the simple declaration that Mr. Mysterious Hadrian was out to enjoy life to the fullest.

He was cute, I had to give him that.

Only the one picture gave me anything to go by. Nice bone structure, shadowy dark hair, a hint of a smirk at the corner of his mouth, but not one that insinuated he was an ass. I couldn't pinpoint his ethnicity either from this lack of information. Not that it mattered, but when you're traveling around a huge international hub like Tokyo, you'll always be curious.

I was intrigued enough to say *Hello* back.

Nothing. Eh, he sent his initial message hours ago, right after I went to bed. He probably thought I was ignoring him. It was time to get up and go about my day anyway.

Lunch (remember, I like to sleep late,) shower, get dressed and decide where I wanted to go work for the day. Thoughts of Ikebukuro lingered in my head. It's one of my favorite neighborhoods in Tokyo, partially because there's so much amazing shopping, but mostly because there are many late-night cafes for this night owl to write in.

It also wasn't too far away by subway. As soon as I sat down on the bench, I opened my phone case and saw an alert from Hadrian.

"*How are you?*"

Wow. He actually messaged me back. Is it sad that I wasn't expecting that at all? Also, I now had to face the fact that I was apparently doing this. For real.

Nah. I always had the right to ghost him or never agree to anything but a friendly chat...

"*Fine, thanks. How are you?*"

His answer was immediate.

"*Good.*"

My day in Ikebukuro pulled my brain in two directions. When I was stationed in the present, my thoughts were clouded with ongoing story ideas and finding a Christmas present for a friend. When I sat down and looked at my phone, however, I only had thoughts for my mysterious match.

Hadrian was a handsome man, or at least the one picture of his face led me to believe that. He was also a man of few words, which may have been a good thing for a guy who would probably end up a one-night stand. Oh, right, when was he going to make a move? Because I had been led to believe that this whole app dating thing basically amounted to "I think you're good looking / I also think you're good looking / Wanna get coffee and or fuck?"

I had no hopes for romance. Hell, my main concern wasn't that he would be *nice*. It was that any potential date I got out of this thing wouldn't go down in flames because the guy turned out to be a misogynistic douchewaffle who thought taking me out meant I owed him my pussy.

I mean, I was *ready to go*, but I still had safety standards!

# Up All Night

First thing I did when I settled down in a café overlooking Ikebukuro Station was respond again. *"What are you doing in Japan?"*

If you've never traveled abroad, or at least never to Japan, then you may wonder why I led with that. Well, dear friends, it has nothing to do with any weirdness relating to me and everything to do with being nosy. We ex-pats in Japan, regardless of where we hail from, always wonder why the hell other foreigners are there. To be frank, Hadrian didn't come across as a guy the local English schools were falling over themselves to hire. There are so few job prospects for foreigners even in Tokyo that it's always the first thing we ask each other. "Yo, man, how did you get a sweet gig here? Is it even sweet? Tell me your life story because I am so homesick, bro."

He didn't respond right away. In fact, it took him long enough to respond that I was deep in my work by the time I saw the blue light flashing on my phone.

*"I work in restaurant. I live here seven years."*

The thing that made me curious *wasn't* his imperfect English, but the fact that he had been here for seven years already and had nothing to do with teaching. That in itself was fascinating... because where I come from, everyone who works in Japan is staying for maybe one, two years tops and is either an English teacher or a translator for some big corporation.

*"Where are you from?"* The Spanish Inquisition had arrived, and it carried the banner "CYNDI."

*"From Greece. You?"*

Ladies and gentleman, I was talking to some hot Greek *gaijin* and the man worked in a restaurant. I had to know more. First, he had finally asked me a real question! Already we had transcended the usual conversation limit before a hookup.

*"I'm from America. Just visiting."*

*"Oh nice."*

Not a damn thing more for a few hours. Great! I had scared him off with my Americanness. Somehow I wasn't surprised. We American women have a reputation for being sexual deviants with huge, scary tits. Some guys can't handle that abroad. (Or at home for that matter.)

I had to get a grip. There was no guarantee that because a guy talked to me he would want to go out with me. At the same time, I was damn new to this. I was used to being the one who asked people out, because for some reason, I was always attracted to those who were either *lazy as fuck* or couldn't comprehend being as aggressive as asking someone out on a date. This is probably why I actually hadn't been on a ton of legitimate dates in my life.

Still, I didn't feel comfortable being the aggressive one when I barely knew who this guy was. I know, I know. He didn't know much about me, either. I *know* I shouldn't have bought into sexist ideals that the guy always asks the gal out first. But, here's a secret. Never, ever in my life has a guy that I am interested in asked me out. If I went out with a guy, I was the one who suggested it first. (Or, you know, we were already hanging out and one thing turned into another…)

I was determined to make this guy work for it a little bit. I may have been on the prowl for a one-night stand, but I had a few fantasies to fulfill while I was at it. Besides, wasn't I playing around at this stage?

Jesus! I needed to calm down!

How the fuck could I calm down when 1) I write sexy romance for a living, and so I am constantly reminded of how people get down and dirty 2) My neighbor was always having sex and making me think about sex, whether I liked it or not 3) This was some seriously rough ovulating happening and 4) SOME HOT GUY WAS TALKING TO ME.

I shut down my work an hour early. My brain was too fried with the sex I wasn't having.

And someone wasn't responding to me. I'd find out why later, but for now, life sucked.

*\*\**

*"I'm sorry. I work late. It is restaurant."*

Should I respond right away, or was that too desperate? I waited ten minutes so he wouldn't think I stared at my phone 24/7 like some loser. I was in Japan, after all. I was supposed to be having a life. (Ha.)

*"No worries. I work late too."*

*"What you do?"*

Oh, boy. My profile said I wrote sexy books for a living, but I suppose that was too intense for someone to read. I wasn't about to believe guys salivated over women's profiles the way we completely deconstructed theirs before deciding whether to respond or not.

*"I write stories for a living."*

*"Really?"*

*"Yup! It's fun."*

*"Yes, it's nice."*

Okay. Cool. It was two in the morning and I had no plans the next day. Was this guy gonna ask me out or not?

I was gonna have to get coy, wasn't I?

Feminine wiles are something I have in spades, although I don't use them often. I mostly put them toward my books – I let my female romance characters act out those crazy wiles that I hoard within me. Even so, I know how to fucking use them. Poor Hadrian was about to be my first test subject in years.

*"Do you have plans tomorrow?"*

God, as soon as I sent it, I realized how fucking transparent that kind of question is! Anyone with half a brain would know I geared up to ask him out.

*"I work. Every day I work."*

Man, was he kidding me!

*"I work every day too. I feel like I always work."* So much for this super sweet and sexy conversation, huh? If this guy worked every day and didn't have time to screw a girl silly, what the heeeelllll was he doing? Jacking off while talking to me?

*"Too sad. We should relax."*

I knew better than to think a "together" was implied there. Live in Japan long enough and you know that "together" is never implied.

Up All Night

***

*"Sorry. I fell asleep."*

I stopped combing my hair as soon as I saw that message. A new day, a new round of my neighbor's bed smacking against the wall while he and his girlfriend moaned their whole lives away. Seemed fitting that I would get a message from Hadrian while this was going on at one in the afternoon.

*"It's okay. You work today?"*

*"Yes. I work."*

*"At the restaurant? What do you do?"* Creeper Cyndi, that's me.

*"I do everything. Sometimes bar. Sometimes cook. Always chat with people."*

No wonder the guy was too tired to talk to me. He did this every day for who knew how many hours? The life of an immigrant isn't easy anywhere.

As much as I liked what I knew of Hadrian, I started to lose hope that we would go out. If he had wanted to, he would have asked by now, right? That's what I thought as I packed up my work things and headed down to yet another café to work on a book that was nothing but billionaires fucking their mistresses. Occasionally Hadrian sent me a message, and I swiped right on a few other hotties, but I already wrote this whole stupid idea off.

Even though I really, really wanted a… date. Yes. Date.

Ladies, you know how it is. Your body is screaming at you to do something, and it's not happy when you respond with a big fat *fuck you, we're going solo yet again.* I would like to personally thank Japan for having detachable showerheads in every shower, but many times it's not enough. Sure, you get off because you know what you like. Sometimes your body is even happy for a few days afterward. Like a man, you jerk off, you move on, life goes on as usual.

And other times you're dying for some actual physical interaction.

Like I said, it had been too long since I last knew what it was like to have a good looking guy fawn over my body and act like I was the hottest encounter they ever had. I wanted kisses. I wanted that look of desire as a man's eyes traversed my body and imagined what it looked like beneath my clothes. I wanted a man to get hard when he looked at me. I then wanted him to fuck the shit out of me as my body finally got what it was screaming for.

This is the fate of a romance author. The lives of our characters are always way more exciting than our own. That's why everything seems so fantastic. They're all personal fantasies to some extent. We take our sexual frustrations and channel them into stories that may or may not make us money. Because if I'm going to be crying for some random dude to fuck me, I better be getting some money to compensate me!

Still, I couldn't get my hopes up. I knew how this worked. I fancied a hot guy, he entertained me for a few minutes… and then said hot guy realized how hot he was and knew he could get someone hotter than me if he put a little effort into it. Unfortunately for me, even though I think I look pretty damn good, I don't fall under a lot of *conventionally attractive* banners and people love making sure I know that.

So far, the only real prospect who had contacted me was Hadrian. All my messages to other men were met with silence, and the only two others to contact me first were Mr. Neckbeard and Mr. Japanese Fetishist. I was on a real roll.

But I guess any good attention was, well, good attention. I counted my blessings as I went about my day and tried to not let the fact that everywhere I went I was surrounded by canoodling couples make me feel worse.

Then I came home. My neighbor? Was on a fucking tear.

I honestly never saw his girlfriend, but I imagined a woman who walked bowlegged because her pussy had been pounded to death. Actually, she probably didn't walk at all. I don't think my neighbor ever gave her the chance to get out of his bed for the past week, let alone actually leave the building.

Must have been nice!

It was the perfect storm of being horny and having the fact that other people have hot, ridiculous sex shoved into my face. If the universe were a person, it was that asshole prep kid at your high school who wears the latest designer wear and always had the latest gaming systems at his disposal. *"Sup, Cyndi? You want this? Well, you can't have it! Hahaha! I'ma tie you up – totally not kinky though, of course – and make you watch me play the latest game you really want for yourself!"*

The universe is a fucking shitheel.

I forced myself to listen to them have one thundering orgasm after another, my body on the verge of a revolt if I didn't get some of my own soon. *They* weren't necessarily turning me on. What was turning me on – and making me so damn mad – was knowing I couldn't get it as easily as these fools could. That I had gone so long without. That the only people who messaged me on a fucking dating app in a city of over eight million people were two weirdos and a guy who was never gonna ask me out even though he kept responding to my messages.

*Fuck* my feminine wiles! Fuck playing even a two-minute game of hard to get! I was going to hit the universe upside the head and get what I fucking wanted!

Some damn hot sex!

"*Hey, what are you doing tomorrow?*" I messaged Hadrian.

"*Tomorrow I have day off.*"

Fucking. Score.

"*Me too. I am taking tomorrow off from work.*" Hint, hint, Mr. Handsome.

No response.

No fucking response!

Today, I imagine him sitting in his room (whatever it looked like,) staring at my message and trying to figure out what I was going for. Now I know that English was his fourth, fifth language, and the way I talked to him may have been too much for him to wrap his head around. Basically, I had broken the fucker.

"*Do you want to meet up for coffee or something?*"

There.

I had done it.

# Up All Night

I had ditched the feminine wiles and pumped that dude full of aggressive American woman. Asked him out. Made my intentions clear. Dude, I only had a week and a half before my period was due, and two days after that I was heading back to America. I had no time to waste!

Naturally, Hadrian didn't get back to me right away. Because that would have been helpful, yeah?

It's usual for the person who asked the other out to feel that moment of crippling anxiety. In real life, you get your answer right away. Either they say yes or no, or they run away – giving you their answer, I guess. Online, though? It's so easy to get ghosted. There's nobody forcing you to reply to someone asking you out. Hell, I had effectively ghosted those other two guys, right? They were gross and totally deserved it, but I still left them hanging high and dry!

It was possible he hadn't seen my message yet. Maybe he tried to interpret it. Maybe he tried to figure out how to tell me no. (Then why were you talking to me, bro?)

*"Ok ye s lets met."*

The man was not great with English, but I didn't give a fuck. I had a date. That thumping bed next door could kiss my fucking ass.

* * *  一期一会  * * *

# Chapter 4

Surprisingly, I knew exactly what I wanted to wear. I had only brought half a suitcase of clothes with me, and the amount I had amassed since raiding Harajuku and Ikebukuro were miniscule. And when you bring so few clothes with you, the world damn well knows that you've brought the best of the best of your nice but comfy outfits.

Dark jeans, plain black V-neck T-shirt that showed enough cleavage to advertise my great rack, and a dark gray cardigan that was *way* cuter than that description makes it sound. Trust me, once I had my hair under control, I was bangin'. Hadrian better think so too.

I'm not ashamed or embarrassed to admit that, unless it turned out I was being catfished or Hadrian gave me some serious creeper vibes, I was going to fuck him. We could go straight to a love hotel room and I'd be cool with that. I wanted sex. The guy being a decent date beforehand? Fuck it, that was a bonus. And I was down for a good date if I knew I would probably get laid later.

That said, I'm also a woman who is a die-hard realist. I know how lots of (particularly young, and Hadrian was a couple years younger than me according to his profile) men operate. I wasn't going to assume he was packing his own condoms around. Seriously. How sad is that? I ain't trusting no man to bring a fucking condom to a date where sex is silently understood to be on the table.

So, being the responsible adult that I was, I left a couple hours early to hit up one of the many pharmacies and convenience stores in my neighborhood to buy some fucking condoms. Just in case, you know.

Here's a tip: Japan does not make it easy to find condoms.

I don't know why, other than it's some government conspiracy to get the birth rate they're always harping about up, but Japan has been notoriously dumb when it comes to contraception. You couldn't even get the pill until a couple of decades ago, and of course that was for "married women." Young people often confess to never using condoms or any other kind of barrier method.

I go out of my way to explain this so you'll understand why I call this the Great Condom Hunt 2k16.

Imagine me, some nobody foreigner, popping into no fewer than three so-called pharmacies and four convenience stores looking for a simple box of condoms. This was all within a one mile radius, mind you. Oh, I thought it would be the simplest thing in the world, even if I didn't find them right away. How hard could they *really* be to find? I even got on my phone and looked it up online, making sure I knew what they were called and what section you often found them in. Because, as you can probably figure out by now, many other foreigners before me had been as perplexed while on the hunt for Japanese prophylactics. Entire webpages were constructed with the intent of instructing and helping dumbasses like me get safely laid.

Problem: pharmacies are fucking bullshit.

What do you other Westerners think of when you hear the term "pharmacy?" Walgreens. CVS. Rite-Aid. Your local mom and pop pharmacy. You know, those places that double as locations to get your prescriptions filled while picking up OTC meds, other health supplies, and maybe some snacks and even *home goods* depending on the size of the place. Bonus! Aisles and aisles of makeup! American pharmacies are notorious for cheap makeup gear that will help you get by in a pinch.

Japan is similar. Except not at all.

From the moment you step into most *kusuri-ya*, which literally translates to "medicine store," you'll notice there is makeup everywhere. Hair care, skin care, everything you could possibly do to alter your body into being more beautiful is available beneath bright lights and chirping J-pop music. Walk two more aisles and you'll find everything you need to take care of your baby while brushing your teeth. Cheap snacks? Yup. They got that.

You know what a lot of so-called pharmacies in Japan are missing? Medicine.

# Up All Night

You cannot get prescriptions filled in Japanese pharmacies. Those are filled in other, much smaller clinics that fill prescriptions and sell you nothing else. Fine. That's how the system is set up in a foreign country? *Fine.* So give me the OTC stuff, Japan! That includes your "family planning" materials!

Good luck finding vitamins. Good luck finding cold medicine. (That shit is so highly regulated you're gonna have to suffer.) Good luck finding some fucking condoms!

I majored in Japanese. A quick vocab search in my electronic dictionary gave me the one word missing from my brain that would help me ask the closest person where the fuck they kept the *gomu*. (Fun fact: they're called rubbers in Japanese too!) Except these pharmacies were so makeup centric that everyone working there was over sixty-five and female. And not the kind, grandmotherly types, either. The kind that would probably balk the moment a foreign woman asked where the hell the condoms were.

I made the executive decision that these places didn't have what I wanted. I'd have to try the convenience stores.

God.

The convenience stores.

Japan is famous for them, isn't it? You can't hear a tale about Japan without hearing all about the ubiquitous *conbini*. I am here to confirm that yes, even out in the sticks where I have lived, you will find a convenience store on every street corner. Sometimes the same company will have stores across the street from each other. Why? Because Japan takes the word *convenience* to extreme. When I lived in Japan as an honest-to-God resident

Cynthia Dane

with bills to pay, I paid them all at the convenience store. While picking up my lunches (that they so nicely cooked up for me) and snacks for the rest of eternity. Did I mention I could also pay my *American* bills from the local Circle K, too?

As it turns out, you can buy anything at the convenience stores, even the tiny ones! Except condoms. You can't buy condoms.

Don't give me that look. I don't care if you could go down to your local 7/11 and point to the small selection of Trojans while waving your arms in my direction. Didn't we go over that the *pharmacies didn't carry them either?*

By this point, I was already running late for my date. Because heaven forbid Hadrian would want to meet in my neighborhood. Nope. Dude wanted to meet six subway stops away in the Oji neighborhood, which I had been to about once in my life.

I reached peak frustration. I didn't want to show up to a fuck date without my own condoms. If nothing else, I thought it might be nice for the poor guy to have a *selection* for his dick. Plus, it was the principle of the thing. So even though I was sick and tired of walking up and down steep, crowded hills to pop into fruitless endeavors, I decided to try one last time.

7/11, if you failed me...

The neighborhood 7/11 was the largest convenience store around. That didn't necessarily mean anything, other than they had ample seating. Yet I held a sliver of hope that this store right next to the train station I needed to hurry to would have at least one pack of condoms.

# Up All Night

My friends.

My *friends*.

I thought the mighty and honorable Amaterasu herself had descended from the heavens to illuminate her sunny light upon the tiny-ass pack of condoms sitting on a back shelf.

One. One pack to choose from, for an exorbitant Tokyo price. I stared at them, convinced that I was hallucinating. It was because I hadn't had dinner yet, right? I was starving, and thus, hallucinating.

Fuck it.

I hadn't come this far to not buy a pack of condoms. I was a responsible adult woman and absolutely mature about this.

Even though the one guy at the register was old enough to be my father.

Most of us have been there. You're popping in to buy condoms, lube, a cucumber... and you think ah, fuck, how embarrassing would it be to buy only this? Because then it looks like I'm running out to get laid right away! Nah, man, I'm going through a list of things I have to restock at home. Condoms, you know? Might as well get some lube since it was right there. I also needed to get a toothbrush, some snacks, and a new umbrella for the missus.

Not that night.

This guy was going to deal with a foreigner marching up to the counter and triumphantly slamming a box of condoms down onto the counter. He was going to give me the same level of Japanese professionalism I was damn well accustomed to, and he was gonna *like it*.

I looked him right in the eye as I approached. I nonchalantly tossed the white box of condoms in front of him and pulled out my wallet. He looked at me. He looked at the box. For a split second, we shared a moment that was nothing short of a struggle for dominance. I wasn't going down with embarrassment first. He could have those honors if he so chose.

Didn't he know that we American women were *sexually aggressive?* Of course we bought condoms and nothing else! Mother fucker, I was about to go get laid because my stupid ass neighbor hadn't let me sleep in a week! This was happening! Some guy named Hadrian was currently en route to our meeting point – ah, fuck, I better tell him I was running late – and I was gonna blow that dick and fuck that cock!

*Now ring up my fucking condoms!*

* * * 一期一会 * * *

## Chapter 5

I emerged from the depths of Oji Station with condoms in my bag and more than a twinge of anxiety in my heart.

This was it. Any moment I would meet Hadrian face to face. I'd hear his voice. I'd see his reaction to me. (Oh, God.) I'd get a feel for how he really felt about me. This was, of course, assuming he'd show up and not run at the sight of me.

(I've been on some pretty shitty dates, y'all.)

Was he tall? Was he muscular? Did he smell good, or did he smell like tobacco like half of the country? Would he be nice, or would he be distant? All I knew was that he was from a completely different culture than what I was familiar with. Would he expect me to be more conservative? Did that mean he wanted to take things slow?

See? I was already bringing myself down before he arr...

I recognized him instantly.

A young man with a spring in his step came out of the subway exit, eyes searching his surroundings before he took shelter beneath a streetlight and checked his phone – to tell me that he was there? To ask me where I was? To message some other chick he had on standby?

I should have approached him right away, but I was stunned. Because he was... *holy shit.*

Hadrian-whatever-his-last-name-was exuded a cool confidence that was anything but off-putting. He stood out of people's way as they passed by, but had a small smile on his chiseled face that was faintly outlined with a healthy and dark goatee. His black leather jacket matched his black jeans and the T-shirt that so casually said *Guy on his day off.* He was the kind of man I would have admired from afar and automatically assumed would want nothing to do with me.

Nope. I was on a date with this guy.

I told myself that as I stepped forward and caught his attention. Thank God, he smiled.

"Hadrian?"

"Yes. You must be..." His face blanked. "Uh..."

"M... uh, I mean, Cyndi." If this guy couldn't remember my fake name, there was no way he was going to remember my crazy German real name. Besides, maybe it wouldn't be bad to be Cyndi for a night! "Nice to finally meet you!" Oops. I was lame.

He immediately pointed down the street. "You hungry?"

I had never heard an accent like his before. I was pretty familiar with Japanese accents when speaking English, and he shared a lot of the same mannerisms, telling me that most of the English he had learned was here in Japan and filtered through that experience. Even so, Japanese could not have been his native language, which made me only more curious about his story.

Assuming I would ever learn it. This was supposed to be a one-night stand, after all.

"What kind of food?" I asked, vainly attempting to keep up with his brisk steps. The guy knew where we were going, and we were going to get there quickly. But how was I supposed to get a whiff of his cologne if we were going this fast through a cold November night?

"Italian. You like Italian?"

Music to my ears, Hadrian! "I love Italian. It's my favorite!"

"Really?" We stopped at an intersection. "It is right there. We go?"

"Hell yeah we go."

The restaurant was practically empty when we arrived. Our young and surly waitress took one look at us and almost rolled her eyes. *"Great. Another couple."* I wondered if she was rolling her eyes at him... bringing another girl to her place of work... maybe she had a crush on him? I mean, *I* had a crush on Hadrian and I was on a date with him.

"You like drink?" He shoved the alcohol menu in front of me. Full disclosure: I'm not a drinker. At all. I never had a sip of alcohol until I was 22 because any outside substance that changes my brain chemistry freaks my shit out. By that time I was more comfortable with imbibing alcohol, but to say I was a lightweight was an understatement. And I *hated* beer, Japan's favorite drink.

"Anything but beer is fine," I said.

"Beer?"

"Anything *but* beer." I needed to simplify my English more. I honestly wasn't used to having this issue with other foreigners in Japan, almost all of whom commanded English like it was their natal language, even if it wasn't. Were Hadrian and I going to have to speak in Japanese to get our thoughts across?

"Okay, no beer." He ordered himself beer and pointed to the wine list as he ordered for me. Oh, great. He probably thought that was a safe bet, but me and wine? Went together only slightly better than me and beer. I loved me some regular grape juice, though.

That also wasn't the only thing he ordered on my behalf.

I perused the entrée menu while he went ahead and ordered us a regular sized pizza, French fries, and a large salad. At first, I thought that was for him. (You know, men and their healthy appetites.) Then the menus were taken away. I hadn't ordered anything.

If you're older than me or from a select few other places even in America, you may wonder why I was weirded out. I had never had this experience before. Not on a date. Never in my life had a man gone ahead and ordered for me. Wasn't that passé back home? I know that in Oregon you would've been smacked up the side of the head if you dared order on behalf of someone you just met – that shit barely flew for people you had known for twenty years.

Then again, this guy was so fine he could've ordered me up some haggis and I would've been all over it. Me. The woman pickier than a cat when it came to her food. Yes, even her Italian food.

Hadrian was already glued to his food when the surly waitress walked away. Awkward.

At first I didn't know what to think. This man had ordered me stuff to consume without consulting me. (Other than asking if I was okay with alcohol.) Now he wasn't even looking at me. Oh, God, I was on one of *those* dates…

His phone was in front of my face. Hello, Google Translate. Apparently communicating with me by any means possible was what was most on his mind.

"*Do you like for the atmosphere like this?*" Well, it was Google Translate…

I looked up at him. "Yes?"

He took his phone back and punched something else into it. "*Please I try my English.*"

"What language do you speak first?" Was that too complicated of a sentence? Was I making things worse? This was supposed to be a nice and relaxing date.

Hadrian has some of the most expressive eyebrows I had ever beheld. They weren't necessarily thick, but they were as black as the hair on his head and moved every time he thought about what I said. I knew that look. Teaching Japanese students English for over a year taught me what that look meant. "*How do I use English? Oh, fuck, what is this American woman saying? They talk too fast! They use too many slang words! This is a pen?*"

Cynthia Dane

"I am from Greece."

"Oh, so you speak Greek?"

"Yes. I speak Greek."

I don't think I had ever met a speaker of Greek before. "You speak Japanese too, yes?"

"Oh, yes, I speak Japanese okay. Not so good, though."

"Bullshit!" He jerked back at my exclamation. "You ordered dinner perfectly. I majored in Japanese. I think maybe your Japanese is better than mine."

Was he blushing? Maybe not, but he had no problems waving away my statement with a shy smile. "No, no, my Japanese is no good. I don't study it. Just learn."

Let me tell you, as someone who has studied Japanese for most of her life, a textbook teaches you nothing. Not like how living in Japan teaches it to you.

"But you speak English. It is the best."

"You think so?" I was used to hearing that. I could never understand why everyone around the world was so obsessed with English (aside from the ubiquity of it, I suppose) but it often explained why my fellow Americans rarely felt compelled to learn other languages. Why bother when everyone else was learning English?

"Yes. I want to learn English most! But... English is maybe... fifth language."

The waitress brought him a beer and me a glass of white wine. "Fifth? You speak four more languages?"

"Yes. I speak..." He counted on his fingers. "Five. Maybe six."

- 42 -

Holy shit! "What do you speak?"

He considered that question before rattling off a list of languages. "Greek, Kurdish, Turkish, Russian, Italian, Japanese…"

"And English! So that's seven."

"I don't speak English. It's not good enough."

Keep in mind that so far we had been speaking entirely in English with only a smattering of Japanese. Damn polyglots. And here I loved to slyly move Spanish into my list of languages even though I am so bad at it now. Shit!

"I think Italian is most beautiful." Hadrian nodded. "Italian, Turkish, Kurdish… Greek is okay."

"I love Turkish and Russian. I listen to music from Tukey and Russia because I love how it sounds." I wasn't lying, either. Check out my Turkish pop music playlist on Spotify sometime. "But I think Spanish is the most beautiful language." I have a problem with it, honestly. It does things to me. Terribly wonderful things.

Yet Hadrian made a semi-disgusted face. "Spanish is not good. Does not sound nice."

"Really?"

"Yes, yes. Italian is more better."

Well, at least he wasn't going on about French. I had a bit of disdain for it at the time.

"Do you study English?"

"I try to speak English when I can, but it is hard to study." He typed into the translator again. I couldn't help but notice he was translating from both Greek and Kurdish. Later, he would tell me he was half Kurdish, his family having immigrated to Greece by way of Turkey. My love for geography got a heavy workout that night – and here I thought memorizing all the prefectures of Japan was an amazing feat. By the end of that night, I had refreshed my entire recollection of not only the Mediterranean but parts of the Middle East as well. "I speak some at work. And Italian. I learn Italian from work."

"Wow. The Italian restaurant?"

"Yes, I work with Italian food. Some…" He punched something into his phone. When I saw it again, it said *"Mediterranean fusion."* Fancy.

"Do you like it?"

"Yes. I want to work with Italian restaurants in America."

"Really?"

"Yes!" Hadrian had a gorgeous smile. The kind that makes a girl hope that he's putting his smile all over her by the end of the night. "Right now I get visa to go to America. This January, I go."

"Wow."

"So I must practice my English. You help me practice, yes?" He drank the last of his beer. I had barely touched my wine. I needed it now, no matter how bitter and sour it was. (And it was quite a bit of both.)

Because let me tell you… "help me practice my English" is the death blow to any relationship in Japan. Ask any ex-pat and they'll give you a ton of stories about how they thought they were on a date or made a friend only to find out they were used for free English lessons. So far tonight, Hadrian hadn't even flirted with me. Oh, he ordered a drink and food for me, but he hadn't... *flirted*. When I thought about it, our messages weren't flirty on his end either.

So for the next few minutes, I tried not to panic. I tried not to fall into the trap of thinking *this guy wants to practice his English on me. He has no romantic or sexual interest in me.* A tad crestfallen. That was me. I needed to shut down any fantasies I had about this man, but they were not going to happen. I had to prepare myself for that, like I had to prepare myself for him acting like a damn man in every area of life *but* the one I wanted.

Which happened when the waitress brought our food over. French fries and margherita pizza? Nice. I could do those. The salad also looked pretty delicious... until Hadrian went ahead and poured the accompanying dressing all over it without asking me first.

I hate dressing. Salad dressing is something that should have never been invented, but I digress. As I had forced myself to do many times when in the presence of new people, I accepted every piece of food, including those I knew would make me sick. I would at least try it, damnit.

(It was as bad as I feared. First, bitter ass wine, and now dressing-drenched salad that made me wanna barf.)

Hadrian tried it too. His face was as bad as mine.

"Oh... oh, it's not good."

At least we could agree on that.

He hailed the waitress and got a second beer. I was still working on my wine without minding how quickly I drank it.

"So what do you do?"

Oh, boy. My favorite question in the whole world.

I don't usually lie about my profession, unless I have a feeling the person is going to be a huge ass about it. I didn't get that impression from Hadrian, but how the hell did I explain what I did for a living to someone who wasn't the best at English? Nuances, you know.

"I write books."

"Books?"

"Yeah. You know, stories."

"Really? As job?"

"Yup. It's my job."

"Wow." That was the reaction I was most used to from people. Most of the world is not used to people making a solid living off writing fanciful stories all day. Let alone the kind *I* write. "What kind?"

Here we went. "Romance. Love stories."

"Aah." Hadrian nodded again. "It's important kind, yes?"

I laughed. "I guess so." The wine got to me. I had every intention of flirting with this guy to begin with, but now? Thanks to Mr. Alcohol, and the fact he dared to say *practice English,* I had no more fucks to give. "I write sexy romance books. Do you know *50 Shades of Grey?*"

His eyes bulged. Apparently, someone did.

"What?" Hadrian nervously laughed. "Yes, I know. You write like it?"

"Yup." I pulled my own phone out of my bag and brought up one of my books on Amazon. "See?" I showed him my bestselling cover.

Up All Night

"Can I…?"

I dropped my phone in his hand. "Knock yourself out." Meanwhile, I was gonna keep drinking this wine. Or knock it over, I guess. My movements were not entirely my own by that point. Luckily, Hadrian was too absorbed in my Amazon profile to give a fuck.

"Wow." He kept laughing, not in making fun of me, but to keep from being too embarrassed to function. "*Wow.*"

I took my phone back. "You ever meet a writer before?"

"No way." He shook his head. "Not like that."

Want to know the other reason I didn't feel shy about showing him what I did?

Yeah, my feminine wiles were back in action. I figured I had one last effort to see whether or not this guy wanted to sleep with me tonight, or use me for his English practice. If I could put any thoughts of sex into his mind? If I could make myself sound like I was down with talking about sexy stuff? That I wasn't shy about two people bonking? Yeah. I would do it. Dude, we were on a date. Flirt with me!

(Unless this wasn't a date, of course. Then he could get embarrassed as much as he wanted. Bye!)

We reached a lull in conversation. How exactly do you follow that up, anyway? Good job, Cyndi.

"So…" I said. "Do you live here by yourself?" Creeper Cyndi returns! In truth, I wanted to gouge whether or not we could go back to his place after this.

His demeanor returned to somewhat serious. "No. I live with my brother."

"Your brother? He is from Greece too?"

"Yes, we came together."

"How long ago?"

"Maybe six or seven years."

"Do you have a big family?"

"Oh, yes. I have four brothers and two sisters."

"Four brothers and two…" Here I was, only-child Cyndi.

"My grandfather had twelve children. My brother has six."

"Wow. You live with all those people?" In Japan? Where the houses could hold maybe four people tops?

"No, no. Only with my brother. Everyone else is still in Greece. Some go to Turkey."

"Oh…"

"Yes." I had no idea what I had unbottled. Hadrian had gone from joking about being drunk off two beers to looking wistfully off into the distance. "My brother and I came here alone. He left his family to make them money."

"I see…"

"Things are not good in Greece. Money is a problem. In Turkey, things are not better for my family. There are bad people trying to…" He furrowed his brows and punched more words into his phone. "*Recruit.*"

Oh.

*Oh.* This had definitely taken a sad turn.

"I hate terrorists," Hadrian said, as if I would ever question him otherwise. Then again, I was American. He probably heard every ounce of shit an ignorant American could throw his way about politics and war. "They ruin everything."

I couldn't argue with that.

From what I pieced throughout the night – because the state of Hadrian's family weighed so heavily on his mind that he often brought them up – his family was a mix of Kurdish, Turkish, and Greek. One part of his family was from Turkey, where unscrupulous characters that I shall not name often tried to forcibly "recruit" adult men into activities said men never wanted anything to do with. The other part was from Greece and still trying to recover from the economic collapse. They had connections here in Tokyo that allowed the two eldest sons to head east to make a living to send back home. How much were they making to both afford an apartment in Tokyo *and* send money back home to their families? And Hadrian was moving on to America so soon? I would argue he'd make even less money, although I wasn't sure exactly what he did. So far I had guessed he was a bartender and not much more.

I felt for the guy. What I had thought was going to be a fun date and possible one-night stand often came back to him talking about his family until he remembered this *was* a date… best to keep things light.

Still, how could I ignore something like that?

"Maybe America will be a good opportunity for you," I said at the end of dinner. I stumbled my way to the bathroom, calling over my shoulder, "Lots of fun to be had in America!" I would know. He could be having a lot of fun in this American.

While I was in the bathroom – and trying to regain my tipsy bearings – I once more pondered how things were going on this strange date. Hadrian hadn't made any moves. He made no references to us going back to his place or to a love hotel. With the language barrier, it was difficult for me to be coy or suggestive. When you're on a date with someone new, you don't want to be so aggressive, you know?

Unfortunately, Hadrian was the kind of guy I *had* to be assertive with. I unzipped my bag and looked at the condoms I scoured my whole neighborhood for. That's right. I had come on this date with the intent of getting laid, hadn't I?

I freshened up and sighed. For all I knew, this strange date was going to end with us going our separate ways right after we left the restaurant. Perhaps it was for the best.

Hadrian was already up when I left the bathroom. Had he paid for everything? Damn. I also wasn't used to that.

"We go?" he asked.

"Sure... where are we going?"

Come on, dude, tell me we're going to a love hotel...

"I want coffee." He went ahead of me. At least I got to look at his sweet ass in those tight jeans of his. It was probably going to be the closest I came to seeing his hot body, so fuck it, I was gonna ogle it the whole way up the stairs. Fuck his coffee, though. I could think of something else that started with a *C* and an *O* that should have been in my mouth.

\* \* \* 一期一会 \* \* \*

## Chapter 6

"This place is busy."

Captain Obvious had already bought me some tea – at least he had consulted me about what I wanted. We were in the world's largest coffee chain, but it being a neighborhood like Oji, the place was small, cramped, and made for people studying or working. Hardly the kind of place two foreigners continued their date. (If that was even what we were doing!)

There was one stool available in the whole place. Hadrian offered it to me while he awkwardly stood nearby, drinking coffee. The Japanese men on either side of me looked askance at us. Seriously, how dare we disrupt their emails?

"Can you see?" Only a few seconds later did I realize Hadrian meant to say "Can you watch?" He put his coffee cup down before gesturing to the bathroom. I nodded. The moment he was gone, I pulled out my phone and found a message from my friend.

Cynthia Dane

*"How's it going???"*

Sighing, I punched in a reply.

*"I have no idea what's going on. He's not flirty. Don't tell me I went hunting for those condoms for no reason. With my luck they're going to be the souvenirs that nobody asked for."*

*"Aw, that sucks. Is he cute?"*

*"Girl, he is handsome as fuck!"* So not fair. I was on this maybe-date with one of the finest foreigners in Tokyo, and I had no idea if this man would even say it was a date! This was actually a history of mine. Men that would never admit we dated, that is. Why would Hadrian be any different at this point?

*"Good luck, girl."*

My friend had no idea how much I needed it.

Hadrian came back the moment two seats opened in front of the window. We claimed them as quickly as our able bodies allowed. Finally, for the first time all night, I was sitting right next to this man, and…

He smelled really, really good. Damnit!

We hadn't sat down for two seconds before a woman passed behind us, grazing Hadrian's back with her purse. He jerked up, startling the both of us.

"Sorry, sorry." He pushed his coffee aside. "I don't like being touched."

Oh. *Oh.* Well.

So this guy didn't do much talking *and* didn't like to be touched? How the fuck did I work with that?

Thanks, universe!

"If someone comes up behind me and..." Hadrian demonstrated a friend clasping his shoulder from behind. "I get... maybe scared."

"Panic?"

"Yes, panic."

I didn't want to ask how something like that came about in his life.

"Sorry to hear that." That meant that, even though I was sitting right next to him, I couldn't slyly touch him with my hand or arm as we talked. Damnit! How was I going to flirt? *How the fuck did one flirt with this guy?*

The universe truly was against me that night, wasn't it?

Hadrian didn't owe me anything. He was nice enough to pay for dinner and my tea. If anything, I would usually be afraid he thought that I owed *him* something. But what a turn of events, huh? The one time in my life I was ready to go – had decided I was going to jump this guy's bones two minutes after meeting him – the guy I was with either played a long game or was totally uninterested. Just my luck, indeed!

"It is lonely, yes?"

I glanced at him. This man with the perfectly groomed head and facial hair, stylish clothes, and polite mannerisms that would make most women fall over themselves like loons. (Like me.) "What's lonely?"

"This country."

I looked out the window. It was the usual sight at any time of day in Tokyo, regardless of the neighborhood. Across the main thoroughfare was the train station. People jetted in and out, alone, no regard for the people around them. Honestly, it was one of my favorite things about Japan. No matter how packed in you were somewhere, people always respected your personal bubble. Funny, isn't it? You could be in the busiest subway in Tokyo, and you didn't care, because the people you were slammed up against were lost in their own worlds. Reading books. Texting. Listening to music. Chatting with coworkers and friends. It wasn't that they didn't care about you. But the way personal space is treated in Japan is simply unprecedented. As someone who spends a lot of her time in public alone, I appreciate it.

"People are always by themselves."

"Yes. They go everywhere alone. Japanese people are always alone."

The way he spoke, whether he realized it or not, was poignant.

"You don't like alone?"

"It feels sad a lot."

I had only known this man for a couple of hours, but I felt like I was learning more about him than I had learned about most of my friends back home. "You like to be around people," I said matter-of-factly.

"Yes! People are best. It's why I like restaurant business. My restaurant, it is food and bar. The bar is my favorite. Everyone is so happy and having a party. It's only time you see it in Japan."

"Well, if you move to America, things will certainly be different."

"I want to move to America," he reaffirmed.

Now that he had opened up again, our conversation turned toward the differences between Japan and the rest of the world. How people were lonelier here than they were in America. How they saw their families less here than in Greece, Turkey, almost anywhere else. How they were more educated than many places we had lived. Oh, and how expensive! Hadrian was shocked to hear that America could be as expensive as Japan, but then conceded that things were also seemingly expensive in Greece even with the comparatively low costs – when nobody could afford those low costs, they were expensive.

"The food is also better," he told me for the third time. "Italy makes the best food. So does Greece. Japanese food is okay, but Italian is better."

"What about American food?"

"American food is good because it has many Italian foods."

I couldn't fault him for that superb logic.

We were laughing about something. I don't remember what. Maybe he told me a joke about his nieces and nephews back in Greece. All I know is that I took that moment of good humor as an opportunity to put my hand on his arm and test his reaction.

He instantly stopped smiling. Not to say he frowned, but my actions had put some damper on the experience. Right, right. He had said he didn't like being touched. I pulled my hand away and kept it to myself.

Hadrian tapped his empty coffee cup on the counter. "We go? Take a walk?"

He had his eyes on the train station across the street. Oh. Good job, Cyndi. You ruined the night and got yourself sent back to your noisy share house.

That was what I assumed as we threw out our trash and stepped out into the cool autumn night. November was a strange time for weather in Japan. One day it would be hot and somewhat humid, and the next it would snow a few inches. That day had been warm, but the night was brisk. Hadrian shivered in his jacket and motioned for us to walk as quickly as possible.

Naturally, we made a beeline for the station.

At least it had been a nice enough evening. My body was screaming at me to fuck this guy, but as far as I could tell, he wanted nothing to do with me like that. Leave it to me to find the one man in Japan not down for a one-night stand. Maybe he was looking for a long term thing and was turned off after finding out I would leave the following weekend. With our language barrier the way it was, it was near impossible to find out the truth.

Not that it mattered, anyway. We were never going to see each other again.

I checked for my wallet as soon as we entered the station. Yet we bypassed the ticket machines and continued to pass beneath the station until we came out of the other side.

Uh, well then!

"This is my favorite park in Tokyo." Hadrian pointed to the paths wandering through the green spaces across the street. "We go?"

"Sure." My attempts to mask my excitement didn't work. This date wasn't over yet? Where were we going? What were we doing? Why did I have to feel like such a teenage girl on her first date? Was I really that sad?

Or was I that... into him?

Whatever. That was silly. The date leading up to any possible sex was that – a date! This guy wasn't going to hold my hand on a stroll through the park. Nor was he going to tell me his innermost thoughts like we had known each other for years. I barely knew him. For fuck's sake, I found him through a dating app! I wasn't going to be in town long enough for us to get to really know each other.

His mannerisms were strange to the point I could barely get a read on Hadrian. He animatedly spoke to me as he described what he loved about this park and how he liked to come here whenever he passed through Oji. Yet at the same time, he kept a respectful distance. I wish I had known more about the culture he grew up in. Was he being polite? God! I wish he would throw his arm around me if nothing else! Touch me a little! I'm not saying he had to slap my ass or try to cop a feel of my tits. Just enough to send me a message that he was into me, damnit!

At the same time, I'm a paranoid person thanks to a lot of shitty experiences, and the fact this guy I barely knew was leading me through a dark park at night sent up the usual red flags.

*At least the guy who kills me and dumps me in the river will be hot?* Yeah, that's how desperate I was.

I never felt like that around Hadrian, though. His unwillingness to touch me – and even talk to me at times – made me more frustrated than comfortable. I wanted to kiss him. I wanted him to pin me against a tree and make a dishonest woman out of me. I wanted him to curl his arm around my torso and hold me to him like he was the luckiest guy in the world. We only had tonight, right? Maybe he was the luckiest guy in the world – he certainly had the power to make me the luckiest gal.

All he had to do was authorize that power. Let me know that it was okay for us to fool around. For me to let down my guards that I erected after I realized this may not be a date.

"Oh, no, I don't like." He stopped in the middle of a path and ducked onto the other side of me. "I don't know how to say in English." His thumb jerked toward a cemetery across the small river.

"Cemetery."

"Yes! Don't like. Protect me, please."

I stopped and stared at the cemetery while he lost the skip in his step. "Why?" Japanese cemeteries are one of the least foreboding in the world. Cremation is the norm there. With no bodies to bury, most graveyards are simple granite pillars with the family's name on them. Personal names of those who have passed on are written in white, while family members who have yet to pass on are written in red. From our distance, all you could see were a few pointed pillars about three feet high clustered together. Hardly anything to worry one's cute head over.

I turned to give him a *look,* but Hadrian's eyes were elsewhere. Namely, on my ass.

Protection, huh?

Last thing I needed to do was playfully chastise or make fun of him. With the language barrier, that was probably not a good idea… and if he were playful right now…

Yes!

"You're cute," I said.

"Cute?" He put one hand on his hip and rubbed his goatee with the other. "It is good thing?"

"If a girl calls you cute, you bet your firm ass it's a good thing."

I don't think he understood a single thing that I said, but his smile was golden. Maybe he was as confused by my signals as I was about his?

We came upon a small wooden pedestrian bridge, the traditional kind that used to be so often found in Japan before the wars. This one was obviously a recent addition, but under the cover of night it looked as if it had been there for a hundred years. I took out my camera and took a picture. Hadrian went to the river's edge and peered into the deep ravine plummeting beneath flood walls.

"It's deep." He said.

"Yeah, think I'll stay back here." I'm a tad hydrophobic. Me and rivers don't get along.

He propped himself up on the fence while I continued to take pictures. The man was practically a monkey while I looked for the best shot with such little light.

"Have too much coffee?"

Hadrian hopped down. "A little bit too much, maybe. Tonight I can't sleep."

I wasn't about to take that as a sign that we were going to have sex all night. (As much as I wanted to.) "Me too. I can never sleep lately."

This was it. This was my last chance to put sex in this guy's brain.

"Why not?" He was by my side again.

"I told you. My neighbor is busy."

He grinned sheepishly. "Yes, you say. Your neighbor has too much..." Here came the phone again. "*Stamina.*"

I nodded. "How can I sleep with my neighbor having so much sex?"

He scratched his head, opened his mouth... and immediately shut it again. Instead, he jerked his thumb behind him. "We go?"

Every time he said that, I had no idea what was going to happen.

We made another loop around the park. My mind ran with possibilities: was he going to ask me somewhere? Would he want to go home? Would he at least try to kiss me in this nice park? I had never had something like that happen before!

No, no, I couldn't get too hopeful. I listened to him rattle about nothing in particular, his words growing faster and his pace quickening without him realizing it.

"Where do we go now?"

"Well, I like karaoke..."

"Karaoke? Oh, I'm not good at karaoke…"

Karaoke is perfect, though! Imagine me and Hadrian in a cozy little karaoke booth where I can use the shadows to snuggle up next to him? Or, you know, he could try to score with a hot woman, if I do say so myself. Karaoke is basically foreplay in Japan.

"Do you have plans tomorrow?"

"Not really." Bullshit. I was going to a concert in the evening.

"Oh, I see. We could go to karaoke…"

I sighed, watching where I stepped in the darkness.

"There's another coffee shop…"

Was it getting colder? It was getting colder.

"We could go to hotel…"

I stopped. "Yes," I said in such haste that I think I gave us both whiplash.

Hadrian likewise stopped. His face was the epitome of *holy shit*.

"Really?" He laughed. "You sure? Hotel?"

"Yes, it's fine."

"Fine? Wow." He turned away, hand on his mouth. When he turned back around again, it was with that false confidence guys love to espouse when they take on the dominant role of a situation. When, you know, deep inside they're crumbling and convinced the world is playing a dirty trick on them. "We go?"

"We go, dude."

On the outside, I was cool and composed. On the inside? *Dying!*

\* \* \*  一期一会  \* \* \*

# Chapter 7

"This one okay?" Hadrian pointed to a nondescript hotel by the station. The quintessential love hotel, where couples with no privacy at home come to do their romantic deeds all over each other. *About fucking time!* I wanted to shout into the parking garage entrance. My body was awake again. "*Oh, hey, we're doing this? Sweet. Let me get horny as fucking hell again. Is this the guy? Damn, girl, this guy is hot! Look at that smile! You gonna get that smile all over our pussy soon?*"

Shut up, body. You're not helping!

"This one's fine." I tried to hide my excitement. After all, I was a shy and retiring young lady who treated this one night stand as the biggest non deal of her life. Didn't want to scare the man off, you know.

Then again, my apparent reservations were not giving Hadrian much confidence. The results, however, were nothing short of hilarious. "You sure? We do this? You okay?"

This man was going to fish for my consent until the end of time, wasn't he? Then again, with his basic English and my coy American attitude, who could blame him?

"Yes. Let's go."

He crossed his arms with a smug sensibility that almost made me lose my shit. Whatever language he thought in, the English translation was clearly, "*Hell yeah, man, you are the absolute shit scoring this American chick!*"

"Okay!" Hadrian uncrossed his arms and marched toward the hotel. "Let's do it!"

He had no idea what that meant in English, did he?

Full confession: I had never been to a love hotel before. Oh, I knew all about them, thanks to common expat knowledge and tales from friends, but actually in one? Nope.

For the ignorant and confused, a love hotel is not your usual hotel. It's a place built around romancing your partner and eventually hitting that home run. Some hotel rooms are perfectly innocuous, and you have no idea you're in one until you find all the porn on TV and the bowls of condoms on your headboard. Usually, though, they're themed. Some of the themes are utterly ridiculous, like "fairy tale in the woods" or "leopard print paradise." You also don't get assigned a random room by the check-in desk. Instead, you pick your own room, where you are presented with previews of the themes and the hourly prices. In the case of this hotel, the rooms were rented for whole nights only.

We stood in front of the LCD panel. About half of them had *Reserved* stamped on them, and the ones leftover were fairly average – if ostentatious is considered average. (No leopard print, though.) Hadrian looked at me and asked, "Which one you like?"

His tone and erratic mannerisms implied he still couldn't believe this was happening. I had broken the man. So, I did what any woman getting ready to bed a hot dude would do: I put a reassuring arm on his shoulder and said, "You choose." He was paying for it, anyway. A consummate gentleman 'til the end!

"This one?" His smile almost blew his face off as he pointed to a white and gold themed room. "Or maybe this one?"

I don't remember what the other room looked like. Because my finger smashed the button for the gold and white room before we could dally any longer. This man had bones in need of jumping, and I had body parts in need of *humping.*

The ticket spat out of the machine. Hadrian snatched it and turned toward the check-in desk, his eyes never leaving my determined visage. "Like that?"

"Like that." I pretended to be completely taken in with the previews of the other rooms while he paid and received the key from the proper-looking lady behind the desk.

The elevator was a tiny, cramped thing that forced lovers into close proximity. I had another one of those moments, as we rode up in silence, where I realized I was about to settle down and have sex with a guy I had barely touched yet. It wasn't the fact that we barely knew each other. I didn't care about that. But so far that night we hadn't as much as held hands. Hadrian made it clear he didn't like unexpected touching. Would sitting on the couch with him and massaging his thigh be unexpected? Would he like that? This man clearly had the giddies for me. As flattering as that was, what were the boundaries? The limits? How were we going to sort this out? We were in a two-person elevator and not even touching!

I let him lead us to the room on the fourth floor. The place was so quiet, so well insulated that there could be swinging orgies going on in every room around us and we would have never heard. Good. I was loud in bed.

The room was exactly as promised in the preview. A decent size, with a queen-sized bed covered in gold and white-threaded blankets that were as inviting as they were awe-inspiring. The pale yellow walls had golden fleur-de-lis stenciled in particular places, while a faux-crystal chandelier glistened from the ceiling. Across from the bed was a huge flat screen TV with a...

Yes, that was a bedazzled karaoke box. It was also the first thing Hadrian pointed out after we took off our shoes and stepped into the room.

"Look! Karaoke! You can use."

What I needed to use was the bathroom. A girl needed to make sure those condoms she went through so much trouble getting didn't get up and run away from her bag.

I came out to find Hadrian sitting on the couch. The way the living area was laid out? The loveseat was pushed up into a corner, and the only way to access it was via Hadrian's seat. He caught my eye the moment I entered, wondering if I should go ahead and take off my sweater.

Fuck it. I was going to sit next to this guy I intended to ride until the sunrise. I flashed him a coy smile as his facial muscles did a ridiculous dance to regain control of themselves.

If you're reading this and imagining two grown adults who were both trying to act too cool in this situation for their own good, well… you would be right. Shame on us!

"Can I sit down?" I asked. Hadrian instantly slid over so I could get a spot on the couch. He sat up straight, mind wound up in rapid thought. Yeah, man, me too. I was going over how I would scoot up next to him and make his fucking night.

He was way ahead of me.

I hadn't sat down for ten seconds before he said, "I want to kiss you."

You know, I was fully aware of what we were going to do that night. The man hadn't paid for a love hotel room so we could sit awkwardly on the couch and talk about our feelings. For us to get this far, he must have been thinking of me. Sexually, of course. Not that I picked up on those cues that night. Hadn't I spent most of the night trying to read his signals and send out some of my own? So much time was spent wasting away in terrible thoughts. Thinking he didn't like me. That he was disappointed with how I looked in real life. That he wasn't into me. That I had completely misread what this date was about – if it even was a date.

To have this man say he wanted to kiss me the moment I sat down? I was shocked. My heart experienced a mixture of joy and wariness. He wanted to kiss me! Wait, that quickly? What about some snuggling? Some easing into it?

"Okay," I said. Okay? *Okay?* Girl…

Hadrian touched my cheek and tentatively gazed upon my beautiful face before…

Before…

Yo.

You ever seen *Bob's Burgers,* also known as the greatest animated show of all time? There's this episode where eldest daughter Tina has a crush on a budding activist and is so excited to kiss him that she doesn't even mind that this boy's definition of kissing is literally inhaling half her face. It's played as a gag on the show, of course. Men (or boys, in this case) can't actually open their mouths wide enough to suck on the entirety of a girl's face. Right?

As it turns out, I have a tiny face, and Hadrian had a huge mouth.

*Jesus Christ floating in baby Moses's basket!*

There wasn't a member of the Bible who could help me when Hadrian literally started playing a game of *suck face.* What I thought was going to be a sweet peck to the lips before gradually turning into something more became something straight out of an alien movie.

Hey, now, that isn't to say I didn't kinda like it.

A lot.

You know why I liked it, even though I could have easily ranked it as one of the worst kisses ever? Because the man had a healthy reserve of passion bottled up inside of him after all. Throughout our date I had questioned whether or not he was into me. In that moment, when his mouth grabbed my face and his hands grabbed the rest of me, I no longer wondered what he had been thinking all night. This man had definitely been thinking about fucking me!

Two things were on his side. First? That I had wanted to fuck his brains out since we started chatting online. Second? That I wasn't big into kissing anyway. A bad kisser isn't a deal breaker for me. Now, a dude who can't fuck a girl right? Get outta here.

Here was hoping Hadrian more than made up for it.

"We go to bed," he growled. Yeah, you read that right. He *growled*. How long had this side of Hadrian been lurking inside of him? How much self-control had he practiced until he felt it absolutely safe to go crazy on me? Because that was the strength of a hundred men yanking me off the couch and hauling me three whole steps to the bed so low to the ground that I had to experience a decent fall to get on it.

I had never been manhandled like that before! It was freakin' awesome!

If I had even the slightest question as to whether or not Hadrian wanted me, I no longer had to wonder. This man was breathing my skin as if he had been yearning to all night. His hands were on my breasts before I had the chance to show them off. When he wasn't indulging in every inch of my body, he attempted to yank his clothing off. Already!

"Wow," he continued to whisper the more he touched and undressed me. "*Wow*."

As much as sex feels good, the emotional validation it offers is almost better than the physical. What's better than a partner who makes you feel like the hottest, most fantastical woman in the world? Few people have been able to make me feel that way. Hadrian was so far up there in such a short amount of time that I couldn't help but wonder if I was his ultimate type. Me! Your average American girl who was a Size 10 on a good day… but at least I had the tits and hips to make it count, I guess. Hadrian was obviously a breast guy. He couldn't get enough of squeezing them through my sweater and was keen on getting them *out* of those clothes.

I took off my sweater. He yanked down my neon yellow bra strap, eyes locked on the writing etched within.

"V… S…"

Really? He was reading my bra strap? When he could be taking off his (and my) pants? "Victoria's Secret," I said. It was one of their best sports bras ever. The comfiest bra in the world! (So, you know, it was immediately discontinued and I will wear them until they literally fray off my body.) "Do you know?"

"No," he said. The strap yanked down my arm, his eager mouth lunging for the tops of my breasts as they emerged from my bra. Yeah, buddy, I sure as hell didn't care about my bra brand either.

Fun thing about sleeping with a man who doesn't speak the same native language as you? The shit they say in the heat of the moment. Was it Greek? Turkish? Kurdish, for fuck's sake? I have no idea. I know the differences between those languages, but I was so drunk on the fact I was getting laid that I couldn't make out any non-English sounds in that moment. I didn't need to, anyway. Whatever he said, the intention was clear. *"You are so fucking hot."*

"You like?" I asked. He must have, because his face was like a kid's in a toy shop when he pulled my bra off and unleashed the mighty D-cups. His next goal was to take off my pants. I wished him luck as he took on my complicated belt and the buttons beneath.

"Yes, I *like*." Growl more, Hadrian! Turn me on until I'm begging you to tear me up! Yank off my pants and fuck me like the man you are! The man who had been such a gentleman up until this moment. Although, as I'm sure a lot of you ladies will agree, sometimes the biggest gentlemen are those who ravage your pussy with your pleasure in mind. (Theirs is a bonus. A guaranteed bonus as long as they're making their lady come so hard her cunt practically rips his dick off his body.) "You're so… so…" He faltered, bless him. "*Güzel kadın.*"

I had no idea what that meant, friends, but I can assure you that it was Turkish. Unequivocally the hottest Turkish I had heard in my life, because I wasn't turned on enough!

This man was going to worship every curve on my body. He was going to growl against my skin and turn into the sort of enamored idiot that makes you feel better about being one as well. Because if he was losing his mind over my disrobement? I wasn't faring much better as he ripped off his T-shirt and showed me his muscular form, chest peppered in dark, curly hairs that begged me to run my fingers through them.

I may have been a little too eager. The man's hands were barely on his belt when I yanked him down and blew his mind with some tonguing. To his ear. His surprised laughter made it worth it.

"You are fun." I don't think I've seen pants come off a guy so quickly. "Can I see?" His fingers were on the hem of my underwear. As if he had to ask.

(The fact he did ask was hot, though.)

"Yes." Did he need help? I could get my underwear off faster than he could blink. Or I could enjoy a man doing it for me. Either way, they were coming *off*.

"Wow," Hadrian continued to say. "Holy…"

Yes. I had a rockin' bod, if I do say so myself. Oh, I've had plenty of shitty dates attempt to inform me that I'm too fat for my own good, but their opinions are far from mattering. I've spent most of my life admiring myself in the mirror, stretchmarks, wrinkles, moles and all. I've got flab. I've got spots. I've got everything most women have and are told to get rid of so men will find them attractive. Well, if this random man I met online could think every curve of my body was the hottest one he ever came across? Nobody's negative opinion mattered! Not from my past, and definitely not in my future… because who gave a flying fuck when I would always have this experience to look back on?

Like the moment his head thumped against my abdomen, his face completely enveloped in what made me *me*. I knew he was getting his fill, all while sticking his hand down his boxer shorts. Come on, man, let me see!

He sat up, drunk on my scent. At least it gave him the confidence / *I don't give a fuck* to pull down his boxers and show me one of the most glorious cocks I had ever seen in my twenty-nine years.

"Sorry my dick is small," he said with a chuckle.

Small! *Small?*

*Sorry my dick is small?!?!??!*

Ladies. *Ladies.*

Bear with me.

Did I not say that Hadrian had one of the finest cocks to ever grace my vision? And, ladies, you know that size isn't all it's cracked up to be. How many of you have dealt with a guy who has a huge cock – and knows it? Half of them rest on their laurels thinking that thing is going to do all the work for them. The other half of the time you're begging for sex to be over so that thing will stop making you hate everything, because it *hurts.*

Hadrian did not have a monster cock. He was hardly a pencil dick, either.

I'm a woman who needs certain, uh, size to be completely satisfied, although the skill of the guy is definitely a part of the equation. I was down for, well, going down on that cock the moment it sprang from his boxer shorts. Know that it was enough to stimulate my imagination while also keeping me from slamming my legs shut in *ah hell nah.*

Basically, I wanted that thing inside of me. Yesterday. God knew my body was screaming for a hot guy to stick his dick in me and fuck me until I begged for clemency. I wanted to take a shot and toast to my shitty neighbor who spent most of my best sleeping hours fucking his girlfriend. Actually, no. He wasn't a part of this picture!

# Up All Night

It was my turn to get some!

Lest we forget I was with a total guy, though, Hadrian must have picked up on what I was telecasting to the universe – because that unwrapped dick sent straight from *God* on its circumcised (and did I mention very, *very* well-groomed) platter was ready to plunge into some greedy depths.

Did I or did I not go on a great condom hunt earlier that day? I didn't have time for these unprotected shenanigans, no matter how many guys thought they were slick as grease going for the bareback experience. Like, I know how tempting my pussy probably looked, dude. How about you not knock me up, though?

"Wait!" Not a word I had wanted to utter that night. Especially with my legs spread open and that tantalizing cock only inches away from giving me what I craved. "We need condom." Yes, folks, when my body is shaking in immediate sexual need, my English takes a crap as well.

"Ah…" I know, Hadrian, that wasn't what you wanted to hear. Tough shit, right? He reached up and grabbed the bowl of condoms on the headboard. "It's necessary, yes?"

"Afraid so."

"I don't like." Nevertheless, he unwrapped one. You know what's hot? Watching a guy grab his cock and unroll a condom over it. Gets me every time!

"Too bad." My legs were still shaking. Pretty sure if he didn't grab my thighs and fuck me senseless soon I was going to riot. How long did it take to put on a condom? "I need it."

"Okay, okay."

That was the thing about Hadrian. He was a total man through and through. Apparently he spent most of the evening planning how he was going to get me into bed. He insisted on playing the role of the provider, including his decisions to order food without my input. He was totally going to shove his dick in me, a random woman he met on the internet, without protection – without even *discussing* protection. I wish I could say he was not the norm… but y'all know how it is with men, particularly younger men. They think they're so slick!

But… and this was the important thing. Even with his moments of total Dude Stupidity, Hadrian never once made me feel pressured. He was respectful throughout most of our date, to the point I feared he didn't like me at all. He sought my confirmation and consent so many times that I wondered if he got off on it.

Later, I would realize how good I had it. Not only that this guy was willing to go to town on me, but that he was hot *and* considerate. How often does that happen in our lives? I'm so used to relaying and hearing my own share of horror stories.

But I digress. You don't care about that. You care about how the man fucked.

Keep in mind that I was so needy that even the most mediocre of men would have satisfied me to some extent. Not to say I was craving a mediocre man. Far from it, friends. What I needed was a man who would give it to me until I didn't know my own name anymore. I needed skill, stamina, and that same gentleman-like quality that said he was sensitive to my needs and pleasure.

So how did Hadrian do?

I may not have spoken many of the same languages he did, but I made sure he got a solid English lesson that night. Namely, I reacquainted him with the Holy Trinity from the moment that talented cock slid into me as if it were fucking meant to be.

I daresay he felt the same way. Why else did he have to latch onto my tits so he could stay upright? Too bad. I pulled him down on top of me so I could suck *his* face off.

Most men start off slow and build up rhythm. So did Hadrian, although I daresay he went from 0 to 60 a *lot* faster than most men do!

I am no wilting flower. I am no shy virgin who doesn't know what her body – or a man's – is about. When my body is craving sex, I know exactly what it needs, and how it needs it. Nothing surprises me anymore. In fact, I would like a few more surprises in the bedroom. For example, I love missionary as much as the next girl, but there are other positions a couple can do to make things, ah, *deeper* between them. Namely, his cock deeper in my cunt.

(You know, that cock that was apparently the most perfect size in the world? Filling me up without any of the discomfort? My body was so fucking ready that lube wasn't on the radar. I had been ready for days!)

"So good…" he muttered on my lips.

"Yeah?" I braced myself against his shoulders. My knees could come closer to my face, right? Because a girl needed deeper penetration every day of the week. "Me too."

That was enough to make him fuck me harder.

This? This was exactly what I needed. I needed a real man who wasn't shy about fucking a girl shortly after meeting her. I needed a guy who had a great cock and wasn't afraid to use it right. I *needed* the sensation of his cock slamming against every part of me, taking me, owning me, sending me into the fucking stratosphere until I knew what it felt like to be *his*. And I felt no shame thinking that. Hadrian had been more than respectful that night. The best way he could continue to respect me and my person now was to fuck it until I came so hard I completely lost my sense of self. Fuck me, use me to get off, make me come, damnit!

"Oh my God!" Was I coming already? From nothing but penetration? Yeah, that's how needy I was that month. From the moment the first of many orgasms hit me, my body made sure that dick wasn't going anywhere. That dick its owner dared to call small!

He stopped, but only long enough to flip me over and pull my ass into the air.

Excellent. My favorite position, and I didn't even have to ask for it.

His hands forced my shoulders down, my face buried in the pillow as he fucked me from behind as hard as humanly possible. Every neuron in my body was on fire. The attentions of this man were going to ruin me. And thank God for that.

I had been fairly quiet that night. Not because I forced a demure demeanor that wasn't natural to me, but because my voice is fairly squeaky and doesn't carry well. More than once

Hadrian had asked me to repeat myself because he couldn't hear me – that and I used English he didn't know, oops. Not now! You should hear me when I'm on the other end of a fantastic fuck. You'd think my soul was ripped straight from my body and sacrificed to angels on high. Yeah, I'm *that* neighbor when given a chance. Eat your heart out, French neighbor guy.

Hadrian, on the other hand, was quiet if not energetic. But I didn't need to hear him roar like a beast when he came. I only needed to experience his fingers pressing deep into my hips and his cock holding even deeper inside of me. It filled me one last time, unprecedented, my body knowing what was going on while my mind begged him to keep going.

"Ah…" He pulled out. I collapsed. "We go, yes?"

I was really starting to love that phrase.

Hadrian threw out the condom and fell down next to me. That hilarious demeanor of smug satisfaction on his face almost cracked me up, but I knew better than to laugh right after sex. With someone new, anyway.

"Very nice."

Oh, no, I couldn't contain it. I grabbed the pillow and stuffed it against my face so I could laugh.

"I shower." Wait. Where was he going? Oh, for fuck's sake, I bagged one of *those?* The kind of guy who rushes to the shower right after the deed is done? I ain't saying I demanded cuddles the moment he came, but come the fuck on. "You go too?"

Well, I guess it was different if he invited me along…

"No, thanks." Girl needed a breather after a roll in the hay like that. Think. Reflect. Assess whether or not she needed to go again. (I did. Oh my God, I did.)

"You sure?" Hadrian had not expected that response. He looked back at me on his way to the bathroom.

"Later." Dude, don't make me feel unhygienic after sex! I don't need that shit.

He disappeared into the bathroom, the water spraying into life shortly after. I remained on the bed, breathless, replaying that excellent encounter in my head over and over. The ridiculous kisses. The way he pawed my body as if he had held back all night. The stupid smiles on his face as he experienced the birthday of his life. (You know, if it was his birthday.) Those kinds of things are what make a woman feel damn good about herself. All I had to do was show up and be myself. Hadrian had done the same thing. What was better than that?

One of my minor fears, however, was that he would come out, get dressed, and bugger off. I prepared myself for that. This was a hookup, after all. Sure, we had a nice date first. But I was under no delusion that he would come cuddle me in bed unless he was up for a round two. With men, you honestly have no idea. At least he was young?

His shower was short. By the time he came back out, still as gloriously naked as a statue of Adonis, I had regained my composure and considered going to the bathroom. Because unlike my neighbor's girlfriend back in the share house, I understood the dire need for a girl to do such things after intercourse.

Hadrian flung back the bed covers and crawled in next to me. He picked up the TV remote and flipped through Japanese channels.

Of course he landed on porn.

"*Iyaaa daaaa!*" the female porn actress cried out while she enacted one of the cringiest scenes you've ever seen. "*Itai! Dame yo!*"

If you don't know Japanese, I'll tell you that these are the types of phrases that get men arrested for assault charges back in America. Unfortunately, they're so ubiquitous in Japanese porn – alongside that face and body language that broadcasting extreme duress – that the first thing out of my mouth was, "Change it, please."

"Yes, yes, don't like."

"*Kimoi.*" Cringey. Creepy. Gross-feeling.

"*Sou. Kimoi.*"

This was probably the first man I ever met who would readily agree with that. I didn't press my luck when he changed it to open heart surgery, though.

Yes.

Hadrian changed our post-sex viewing to fucking *open heart surgery*.

(I don't take medical shit well.)

"It's interesting," he said.

"Really? You like this?"

He didn't push me away when I cuddled up next to him, hand plucking a few curly chest hairs. "Yes. Science is interesting."

I was grossed the fuck out, but this was still better than distressing porn. Besides, I could ignore it and focus on him instead.

Hadrian changed the channel. Western porn. Well, soft core porn. That was one curvy blond woman shaking her ass at the camera, anyway.

"Oh, this I like!"

I couldn't help but laugh. "You like that type of woman?"

He waggled his eyebrows at me. "It is the best."

"You ever date an American woman before?"

"No, not before you."

"Really? So? What do you think?"

He bit his lip, eyes wandering as he collected his thoughts. "It's nice. I like."

Good answer. "That's why you want to move. You want to date American women."

"Ahhh… maybe?"

Well, ladies, you're welcome. Because of my great and terrible sacrifice, hunks like Hadrian are encouraged to move to America to sex us up with their talented cocks and great-smelling cologne. (Tip: Don't get offended if they run off to the shower afterward. You were so much woman they needed a little time to themselves.)

The channels finally settled on a news report. The same one I had seen a million times that month: some woman was out there getting busted for growing weed, which is one of the biggest scandals possible in anti-drug Japan. Still, I'd take that over porn and open-heart surgery, thanks. Renewed with

Hadrian's flirtations, I slipped my hand down his stomach and teased his abdomen. He continued to bite his lip and regard me with curiosity.

Finally, he laughed, throwing back the covers. "Yes! Touch my dick!"

Confession: I find guys who say dick during sex to be absolutely hilarious for all the wrong reasons. But when Hadrian said that with such excitement, well, I had to touch his dick!

Aaaand not just with my hands, although they were pretty busy too.

I've already told you that Hadrian had one of the most beautiful cocks I had ever seen. Since making that assessment, I made it my duty to get a closer look at that thing that brought me so much sexual relief in my time of hormonal need. And maybe give it my personal thanks with a kiss or five thousand.

"Is it okay?" I asked, my intentions so clear that I daresay he wondered why my mouth wasn't already on him.

"Yes, *yes.*"

My God. What a dick.

I had never in my life had that thought with a side of positivity. But what the hell else could I think once my mouth was on that thing? I don't care what Hadrian thought about his cock. I worshipped that thing like it was made for my mouth to suck and my tongue to tease. The whole length of it was so satisfying to kiss that I cursed biology for not letting this man stay hard for the rest of my fucking life – or at least the night. I would have sucked Hadrian's cock for the rest of my trip even if I knew it would never go in my cunt again. Honey, it was *that* good.

(Did I mention the man clearly shaved or waxed the business down there? Because he did. I was shocked. And pleasantly surprised. Made everything ten times better!)

"You like?" I asked with a kiss to his tip.

You should have seen his face. "It's perfect."

Hear that? I was fucking *perfect!*

Hadrian flopped onto his pillow and covered his face with his hands. No wonder. That totally-not-small dick grew rock hard beneath my hand and mouth. I would have taken him to completion, but then my thoughts turned to... if he came, would he be able to fuck me again? Probably not! Fuck that!

"Okay," I said with a grin. "That's enough for you. What are you going to do for me?"

I don't think he understood a word I said, but he got the message. "We go again?"

"Fuck yes we go again. What are you waiting for?" He was hard again! Get in me! There were more stars to see!

He flipped me onto my back again, that playful demeanor too much for my poor heart to bear. Hadrian covered me in eager kisses that had gone up in sweet quality since we briefly made out on the couch. I grabbed his hand and directed it between my legs.

"I touched your dick? Now you touch my pussy." A girl had to make sure she was ready.

The man was as relentless with his fingers as he was with his hips. I think I broke his brain when I told him to take me two fingers at a time. Oh, let's be real. I broke his brain about ten times that night.

"Wow." The more he gasped in awe over my body and what it could do, the more I loved it. "*Wow*. So hot."

Did he mean the act itself or my insides? 'Cause I'm sure both were true.

He kissed me again. The news reports continued to play on the TV, and I didn't give a fuck. "I need you." Hadrian's voice was as raspy as mine by that point. "I take you. Now."

I was not saying no to that. Because, funny, I had been hoping he would say that. And I didn't even have to tell him to get a condom this time!

The second time around was more intense than the first. With the driving desire for sex out of our systems, we were able to achieve a more intimate moment now. And by *more intimate*, I mean he was more attuned to what my body did and I completely lost myself to the undulations of crazy sex.

This was it. I knew this was going to be the last time tonight. For all I knew, it would be my last time with Hadrian. Maybe my last chance for sex with a guy for months. (Hey, you never know!) I had to make the most of it. I had to enjoy every second of it, because even though Hadrian was young, he probably wouldn't be able to go a third time. I probably pushed it with a second time as it was. I know that his breathing was erratic and his movements so deliberate that he pushed himself to new limits.

"Come here." That was the only thing he said in English. Everything else was a mixture of Japanese, Turkish, Greek,

Cynthia Dane

God knew what. Whatever phrases in whatever language that popped into his head was an instant lesson for me, the woman enjoying every hard thrust and grip to her body. I might have enjoyed it a little too much. Because the only time he spoke English again was when I moaned so loudly he was compelled to stop and ask, "Are you okay?"

"Yes!" I sounded like a dying cat, but my pussy was dying because of how *good* he was, all right? "Don't stop!"

He did one better. He lifted my legs to give himself the deepest penetration possible. Bonus? He looked me right in the eyes, his glossy brown ones so consumed with lust that I couldn't help but moan like that again.

I watched him come before I felt it.

Men don't often show us their vulnerability. This goes for men all over the world. Perhaps I've seen more of it back home than I have abroad, regardless of the guy's ethnicity or nationality. But when they come like that? And let you watch? Doesn't matter if this guy is yours for only a night or for the rest of your life. That's fucking special. It also ensures you're never, ever going to forget him – and he'll probably never forget you.

Hadrian flashed me a wan smile before slowly pulling out. I should have enjoyed that moment a little more. Because the look of panic blowing up his face once he looked down kinda ruined everything.

"Shit!" He ripped off the condom and tossed it in the trash before I had a chance to figure out what happened. "Come on! Shower!"

## Up All Night

It wasn't until I was halfway across the room, my poor body addled from sex and my brain fritzed to hell and back, that I realized the damn condom had broken.

* * *  一期一会  * * *

## Chapter 8

The hot water hit me the moment I entered the spacious shower. Hadrian didn't bother to rinse himself off first. That detachable showerhead was immediately directed at my thighs, and it wasn't with the intent of bringing me pleasure.

In fact, me having another orgasm would've probably been a bad thing. Those contractions suck the swimmers up, you know!

Now, I kick myself. Of course the condom broke, you idiots! Since when are the one-size-fits-all (ha!) condoms left around love hotel rooms gonna be big enough for a guy? Condoms run small in Japan. Hadrian was such a fucking piston that it was only a matter of time before a condom broke!

God, *why* didn't we use the ones I bought? They were still in my bag! Wow, dumb!

*Good job, girl.* That's what I thought as I sat on the edge of the bathtub and received the shower of my life. Hadrian wasn't leaving anything up to chance. He looked to me for the briefest consent and plunged his fingers into me, making sure everything washed out.

Damnit, why did it have to feel good, too? Fuck my stupid body that was so hormonal I was probably going to get pregnant based on principle.

Fuuuuck.

Hadrian finally rinsed himself off after fingering me for protection's sake. I occasionally accepted the showerhead into my hand and directed it at my thighs. Damnit, what was the point? Damage was done. But whatever gave him peace of mind, I guess.

"You okay?" he asked after handing me the showerhead a final time. "I finish."

"Sure." My mind was still reeling. The date. The sex. The stupid condom breaking and ruining everything. Bet my stupid neighbor didn't have to deal with this shit. "Thanks."

He wasn't smiling when he grabbed a towel and left the shower. I remained there, sighing, wondering what my odds were that I was going to end up pregnant from this. I had been through such a dry spell with guys that I wasn't on any kind of HBC and never got an IUD. The condom was the only thing standing between me and pregnancy. With a one-night stand? Really? I'd be far from the first woman, but why *me?*

Might as well take a full shower while I was in there. The mood was officially over. I fully expected to walk out of there and find Hadrian dressed and ready to leave. The guy had accidentally came in me. That rooster was going to fly the coup before this hen could hatch an egg on the other side of the world.

Hadrian was not getting ready to leave by the time I left the shower, towel wrapped around me and attitude curiously calm. He was even still naked, lying in bed with the remote control in his hand.

Huh.

"Okay?" he asked me. That was certainly a concerned edge to his voice. Was he inquiring after my wellbeing? Or was he concerned that he was going to be a daddy like his brother was a daddy to... how many kids? Five? Six?

Hadrian may have almost been thirty and supposedly childless, but damnit, he wasn't ready to catch up yet.

"Yes. Okay." I climbed in next to him. "Don't worry. No baby." There would be no babies, damnit.

"You sure?"

"Yes. Don't worry about it." Hey, I decided not to worry about it. What was worrying going to do for me? I was still here tonight with a man I had a good time with. We had this room for the whole night. I didn't want the mood ruined, but...

Apparently, what I said relaxed Hadrian enough to let him close his eyes. "Okay. No worries. I sleep."

Typical man, ladies and gentlemen.

I may have been severely lacking sleep lately, but I was too wired on caffeine, sex, and a broken condom to join him in snoozeville. So I messaged my friend and told her what happened, all while flipping the TV channel to a hilariously dubbed episode of *Criminal Minds*.

# Up All Night

*"What happened???"*

*"The condom broke."*

*"Holy fuck, girl."*

*"At least it was worth it?"*

Hadrian snored.

I pulled the covers up around my chin. Maybe I should try to sleep. This was the first night I had in a long time where sleep was guaranteed. Not like Hadrian snored *that* loudly...

I must have slept a little bit, because when I rolled over, the channel had changed, and Hadrian was awake again.

"You okay?" I asked.

"I'm okay. Can't sleep."

Dear friends, I wish I could tell you that we spent the whole night awake because we couldn't keep our hands off each other. I wish I could relay some of the more poignant things he talked about, namely what was on his mind with matters back home and his upcoming move to America. I didn't talk much about myself. There wasn't anything I wanted to say on a night like that, and anything I *did* have to whine about wasn't anywhere near his level of worry.

I was a woman on vacation. Hadrian was a man still trying to find his place in the world, wherever that place was. It hadn't been Turkey. Or Greece. Maybe not Japan.

But we did stay up all night. I forewent catching up on some much needed sleep so I could listen to him gush about his family, what he loved about his job (and what he didn't,) the differences between Japan and Greece... he showed me music videos of his favorite artists back home, I confessed that I am obsessed with Turkish pop music (nobody he liked, of course, but we all can't be huge fans of Hande Yener and Gülşen) and he told me that one of the reasons he had to leave his home country was because he was on "a list." Because he protested the regime that had moved into his home – and because that same regime tried to make him one of their own. It was so eerily close to other moments in history that I could only shake my head. What *can* you say to that? Especially when I try to stay abreast of what's happening around the world, but there are obvious blanks in my worldly knowledge.

And especially since we were in bed. Naked. And we barely knew one another.

"I go to America," he said with more conviction. "If I can make more money in America, then I can bring my family to America. First I bring my brother so he can make more money. Then I bring his wife and children. Then I bring our parents, our other brothers and sisters. Brother's wife's family. My sisters' in-laws. Everyone we know will come to America."

"Good luck," I told him. "It's hard in America, but I think you can do it."

"Japan is hard. America will be hard. Everything is hard, but we survive, yes?"

It's those sorts of statements that put a lot of your own troubles into perspective.

I was endeared to this man that I barely knew. I wouldn't say I was in love with him, goodness, but I had already decided I wanted to see him again before I left. Not just for the great sex, but because talking to him was more mentally stimulating than most of the other foreigners I met in Japan. I suppose that went for me as well.

I had no idea how to take it when he got dressed at five in the morning and bent down to kiss me goodbye.

"Sorry, I need to go." His thumb lingered on my brow. "I use phone later. Message you."

I didn't believe him, but it was nice of him to give me that little bit of hope. This was a one-night stand. He knew I was leaving soon. He had his own plans to make. I was probably his last real fling in Japan before he went off to America to try to make his dreams come true. What else could I do besides cling to my fond memories and hope that he would message me again?

He wouldn't. I knew he wouldn't. Yet I said, "All right. Talk to you later," as he went over the brief checkout procedure and told me to finally get some sleep.

Hadrian left a closed-off man. Me? I was opened up in more ways than one. I was also going to suffer from a serious lack of sleep yet again.

At least this time it was worth it.

* * * 一期一会 * * *

## Chapter 9

There were no messages from Hadrian the next day. I went back to my share house, changed, took a nap, and went off to my concert with a mixture of feelings that I couldn't put words to. Here I had one of the greatest nights with a man I would probably ever have in my life. He was *hot,* multilingual, driven to succeed, and so damn respectful that I was afraid he wouldn't give me what I wanted (nay, needed) in the bedroom until he proved otherwise. He didn't treat me like a piece of meat. He didn't scare or threaten me. If anything, he was the consummate modern day gentleman. And he was gone.

Sigh. Even now, thinking back on that surreal day where I went about my business and enjoyed other facets of my life, I get this strange sense of foreboding. I was still the same Cyndi. Nothing had changed in the sense that I had gone through something brand new to my life, although finally getting what I wanted was a nice change.

No, what kept me hung up on Hadrian was the overall experience. That glimpse of life that slips through your fingers and makes you wonder if you'll ever come close to that again.

So I wasn't quite over him yet. Can you blame me? You read about my date and the great way he loved on me, even if he didn't love me. And since this is technically a romance novel, you know how it's probably going to end.

Yes, folks, this is the part of the story where I hate everything and am convinced I'm never gonna have love again.

But I'll spare you the angst and drama by telling you it lasted about a day. Because if we're going to have our happy Romance ending with only a week to spare, I gotta get over this shit quickly!

It also helps that I got a message from Hadrian around eleven that night. Do you know what it said?

*"I'm sorry because last night. The room air is hard on my throat. I cough a lot."*

On one hand, the air was dry in that hotel room, yes. On the other? Ha! Bullshit, dude!

Of course, I wasn't going to tell him that. *"It's okay. I understand. How are you today?"*

Because I wanted to see him again, duh. Might as well segue him into it.

*"I am okay. You?"*

*"I am also okay."* You know, I read back these messages I have saved on my phone and think... God, we're so lame! *"I had fun last night."*

*"Me too."*

I waited a few minutes. Odds were he was at work. But did he know how badly I wanted to see him again? How much I wanted to nestle my head against his chest and inhale that intoxicating cologne? Aftershave? Whatever it was? How much I wanted one of his terrible kisses? How I yearned to feel him on top of me, behind me again? I was so pathetic, I even fantasized about sucking his cock again. Hey, if you saw and felt that thing, you would be fantasizing about it too! Hell, I wanna do it right now!

*"Should we meet again?"*

*"Yes, again. Me too."*

*"When is good for you? I leave next weekend."*

Trapped in my room that night with nothing but my mind to keep me company (my neighbor had thankfully toned it down on the sex for a couple of days. Probably had his dick in a splint,) I agonized that he was never going to answer me, even if he was busy at work right now. As a child of the '90s, I grew up with these images of women waiting by their phones, their answering machines, anything that would create correspondence between her and that mystery date from the night before. Was he going to call? Would it be uncouth if she called first? Well, as an older Millennial and a child of the '90s, I can safely say I grew up to a different world. With instant messaging, we don't have to turn each other down face to face. Hell, we don't even have to say anything at all. True, people could have not called back then, but now it hurts even to think about how *easy* it is to contact people… and never do it.

Basically, the son of a bitch ghosted me.

# Up All Night

For *days!*

I was a nervous wreck those first two days. Why wasn't he answering me? Did he change his mind? It had been two, three, four fucking days. At first I told myself he was working late and needed to sleep through the next day. Fine. Whatever. He'd get back to me, right? Anytime now. I'd be at dinner, at a café writing, on the subway playing Neko Atsume between stations, doing *anything* in my day to day life when he would finally contact me again. Probably with another apology.

Except he didn't.

After the second day, I stopped checking my phone every fifteen minutes. I had to stop living like that. I had shit I needed to get done. People to see.

Illnesses to fucking have.

That's right, folks. Yours truly got sick two days after seeing Hadrian. See, there was a plague in Japan. A coughing, hacking, wheezing plague that completely knocked you off your ass with a fever for a day and then, if you were oh-so-lucky, made you hack up your lungs for days afterward. Now, I had actually been a little sick with the same thing a couple weeks ago. I felt so terrible back then, because of those thin share-house walls, but now I didn't give a fuck as I suffered with my even worse relapse. I would cough as loudly and proudly as I possibly could when my neighbor went back to his fuck-a-thons.

I was particularly proud when one night he woke up at 4 am and cried, "*Nemurenai! Minna urusai!*" Loose translation? "*I can't sleep! Everyone's too fucking loud!*" Good. Eat your god damn heart out, you French asshole.

I was miserable in more ways than one, and this piece of shit was going down with me.

So there was pitiful little me, hacking up both of her lungs all day, every day, staring at her phone wondering when Hadrian was ever going to get back to her. If ever. Meanwhile, the only reason I got any sleep at all was because I was that knocked out. Although my neighbor continued to fuck his way through the night and occasionally wake me up. Whenever that happened, I made sure to cough harder to spite him.

By the end of the third day, as I sat in my favorite restaurant reading my next installment in billionaire fuckathons and wishing I got some of that of my own again, I made the decision. An important decision that I'm sure you've been screaming at me to have by now.

If I didn't hear from Hadrian by the next morning, I knew I was never going to hear from him again. I had sent him one last message, restating that it would be nice to see him but I was leaving in a few days. After that, I stopped checking. I still got hopeful whenever I picked up my phone for other reasons, but nope. Nothing. And I knew there would be nothing, because the asshole had ghosted me.

Why? Why do guys do that? Was Hadrian merely leading me on so I wouldn't think he was an asshole until the time was right? Or had I scared him off by acting too needy on accident? A million scenarios ran through my head. He hadn't actually liked me. He liked me too much but didn't want to get too deep with a woman who was leaving – or because he was leaving. There was someone else. He had been lying about everything and didn't want to face his lies. He was so busy he completely forgot about me. Honestly, that was the least hurtful one.

No. No, I had to stop those thoughts. So I told myself that if he didn't get back to me by the next morning, he never was going to, and I had to move the fuck on!

Maybe find another date? Ugh. No. Not worth it. Besides, any man I went on a date with? I would compare him to Hadrian, for better or for worse, and I didn't need that shit on my soul.

But even though I had accepted he wasn't going to return my message, let alone in time for us to meet again before I had to leave, that didn't mean my attitude was awesome.

Would've been one thing if I was only dealing with being ghosted. Being sick on top of that? Blech. But you know what was worse? You know what the one thing that made me really hate my life was?

If you guessed *my shitass neighbor,* then you are correct! That fucker could still go to hell!

We were back to our regularly scheduled sex marathons next door. Every two hours those two were back to fucking. The bed smacked against the wall, knocking shit off my desk. I hated everything because nothing I did blocked them out and let me sleep. My lack of sleep kept me sick longer than I should have been. I spent so much time wanting to put a bullet of mercy in my brain that it should be no surprise that I swore vengeance upon them and every little sperm that man had ejaculated over the past two weeks.

Cynthia Dane

It should come as no surprise, my friends, that I received a message from you-know-who when I was in the middle of a sleepless night thanks to the worst neighbors a girl could ask for.

*"I'm very sorry. My phone break. I get new one. You in Japan?"*

I couldn't believe it.

I couldn't fucking believe it! The bastard was back online! And daring to talk to me!

My gut instinct told me to believe him. After all, he had gotten back to me, hadn't he? Maybe the thing about his phone was true. Maybe he really had broken his phone, and one of the first things he did was message me.

I wanted to believe it, okay?

Ladies, you know what I did. Come on. I don't have to tell you that I didn't immediately message him back. That would've been weird, right? So I waited as long as I could without fear of him going to bed. A whole twenty minutes. That's right. I kept that fucker hanging on for a whole twenty minutes! HA! Can't be tamed!

*"Yes, I'm still in Japan. Sorry about your phone."*

Come on, Hadrian. Last time you made me ask you out. Could you ask *me* out this time? You know I'm game to fuck you. I wouldn't still be talking to you if I had such a miserable time, and I think you and I both know that I had fun that first night we met.

*"What you do tomorrow? Work?"*

I did have plans to work on a novel the next day. However, I was willing to change any plans if it meant seeing Hadrian.

"*No plans.*" Yesssss, that would make him ask me out! Don't complicate it, girl!

"*We meet tomorrow?*"

Spike it in the end-zone! Go out for celebratory drinks! Slam dunk that mother fucker! Pound my hands against the wall I shared with my shitty neighbor and scream, "*It's my turn, asshole!*"

What I meant to write was, "*Sure! What is good for you?*"

He told me he had to do something in the afternoon and that dinner would be best. I agreed. I needed some time to get whatever beauty rest I could and get ready for my big date with Hadrian, the comfortable-with-you edition.

What we didn't agree on was where to go. He said he was fine with anything, or that we could go back to Oji. Me? I sat there, listening to my shitass neighbor nut-off in his girlfriend for the third time that night and typed, "*Why don't you come to my neighborhood? There is a nice restaurant here.*"

"*Okay. I come to you. Last time you came to me. It's good.*"

I think he meant to say that it was fair, but whatever. Point was? I was concocting the plan of the century, and I needed Hadrian and his awesome cock to do their parts, if you know what I mean.

"Yes!" my neighbor cried while his girlfriend remained as silent as a mouse yet again. "Nice!"

You keep thinking that, buddy. Because I was about to *get even.*

* * *  一期一会 * * *

## Chapter 10

Problem: I had no idea where to take Hadrian for dinner. I agonized over that more than I agonized over what to wear.

If I were a decent cook, I would have made him something at the share house. But I can't cook worth shit, so a restaurant it had to be.

My neighborhood had a ton of restaurants. A lot of them were nothing special, though. A lot of chain restaurants you find in every neighborhood in Japan. A ton of Italian restaurants that a connoisseur like Hadrian wouldn't find special for a date. There were a lot of Chinese and Indian restaurants that I'm sure were perfectly fine, but I'm so finicky about those cuisines that I wasn't sure if I could handle them.

The only thing notable about my neighborhood was the plethora of French restaurants, but again, a cuisine I didn't really jive with. Besides, most of them closed early in the evening, so that didn't do us any good.

# Up All Night

I got lucky when I canvassed the neighborhood that afternoon and found an "American" restaurant ran by a couple of foreigners. (They even spoke English. Whoa.) Although I wasn't that worried about getting Hadrian to a restaurant. I was more worried about what I had planned for later that night. I hadn't told Hadrian what I wanted from our last night together. I mean, I wasn't going to trick him into anything. Goodness, no. But it was going to take some awkward conversations for him to understand what was up.

First, dinner.

I met him outside a nearby train station. He still wore the tight jeans and leather jacket, but his shirt was a long-sleeved turtleneck that made him look so stupidly good (that's a real description, yes,) that I convinced myself every woman walking by us was jealous of me. They had to be. Look at this handsome devil approaching me with a smile and a pat to the arm. Look how comfortable he is with me. Look at how he *kisses my cheek!!!* before staying a respectful distance away from me as we walk down the street. He could hold my hand or loop his arm around my shoulders any time he wanted, but I wouldn't ask it of him. That would've been something he worked his way up to over multiple dates.

Too bad we wouldn't have them.

"You like American food?" I asked.

"American?" What was that face for? Was he going to question what "American" food meant? (You know what it means in a foreign country. Hamburgers. Good ol' fashioned types of hamburgers. If you're really lucky, you get a place that also serves up American breakfasts and dishes like country fried steak. If you're lucky. You are rarely so lucky in Japan.) "Yes. I like American food."

"Good. Because if you're moving there, you better like it." I could've said the same thing about Japan and me, oops. There's a reason I always lose weight in Japan, and it has everything to do with the fact I can't eat much of the local cuisine.

"American food is good. Although Italian is better."

"You know, I can't argue with that."

The owners of the restaurant waved at me when I brought my date in. The Canadian woman in charge gave me a knowing wink as she handed us English menus. Hadrian instantly gave his menu the most puzzling of looks, so I quietly asked the woman to bring us one of their Japanese menus. She was surprised, but said nothing.

"But I need to practice my English," Hadrian said.

"You can look at both. It's best way to practice Japanese?"

He smiled. "Maybe so."

Good thing I got him a menu he could better understand, because the burgers there were, uh, intense. They allowed you to put almost anything and everything on a burger. Some of it was very American, like bacon and "house sauce," but other things were hilariously Japanese, like extra octopus ink and pickled ginger. No thanks to both. I would, however, try a bacon burger for the first time in Japan. Do you know how hard it is to get bacon in Japan? It is *not* something they consume on a regular basis, even though pork is the second most popular meat after fish.

Up All Night

Once we placed our orders of separate burgers and a giant basket of fries to share, the owner left us to our little corner. I admit, I was a bit nervous to have this date within earshot of others who spoke both English and Japanese.

"Again, I'm sorry about this." Hadrian showed me his new phone. "It break. I get new one. I message you but too long."

His panicked face told me that he feared I would be angry with him. Honey, if I were that mad at you over something so silly, I wouldn't have gone out on this second date with you. "No worries. I understand."

He sighed in relief. "I'm glad. I think I want to see you again. You ask me to see you. I am happy, but something like this… it happened."

I nodded. "Maybe I worried a little. Like maybe you didn't like me."

"Really?" He laughed, opening the translation app on his phone. He punched something in before showing me the screen. *"You are impossible not to like."*

I blushed. I mean, really! This guy was going to lay the flirtations on heavy tonight. Good. He could make up for last time.

"You go back to America?"

That was what he was going to start with? "Unfortunately. I don't have much choice. I have to go home."

"Ah, it's nice. Home in America."

"Soon it will be your home too."

"Yes. I leave in…" he counted on his fingers, "three weeks. So soon. Also too far away."

"It'll be here soon enough."

His demeanor implied he had no idea what I said, but he would smile anyway.

You ever get the impression that some people really, really want to be around you? Not in a creepy way, but for some reason they're taken in with you (before they really get to know you, unfortunately) and spend the next two weeks finding excuses to be near you? Obviously the exact opposite seems to be more common, but it's the ones who like being around you who surprise you the most. In the case of my dear Hadrian, he couldn't stop smiling to the point I wondered if he knew where his usual brain had ran off to.

"You are very pretty today... uh..." He looked down at his phone. "Cyndi."

Oh, ouch. Not the pretty part, but the part where he was still calling me by the wrong name. Perhaps I should have fixed that before going on a second date with him. But my real name is so hard for Japanese speakers to say. Granted, Japanese isn't Hadrian's native language, so who knows what sounds are hard for him to say.

"Actually..." I cleared my throat. "My name isn't Cyndi."

"Yes, you say before." He flicked the napkin beneath his fingertip. "Can you tell me?"

"What? My real name?"

"Yes. Please."

I don't know why he wanted to know. This was the last time we were ever going to see each other, so what was the point? "Mildred."

He stared at me. "Mi... Mil..."

God help me, I have one of the most Germanic grandma names possible. If Hadrian couldn't wrap his tongue around it, imagine how Japanese people, who don't have Ls or Rs in their language, fare! Can you blame me for picking a name like Cyndi for my romance writing career? Sheesh. "Mildred." Did I dare to say it how it's spelled in Japanese? "*Mi-ru-do-reddo.*"

"Oh... it's difficult. You have nickname?"

"Nope." I hate variants on my real name. Milly. Like, really? Someone once thought they were cute trying to call me Milda. Milda! "Sorry. You can call me Cyndi if it's easier." I'm not used to hearing that name in real life, but here we are.

"I like your real name. But, it's difficult to say."

"I understand. Not like yours. It's easier."

"Yes, but Japanese people have difficulties."

I could only imagine. *Ha-do-ri-an* is how you would say it. One of the only good party "tricks" I know is writing people's names in Japanese.

"So where will you work in America?"

We received our food, which gave Hadrian enough time to come up with an answer. "Restaurant. Italian. With friend."

I figured it was like how he got his job here in Japan. A friend knew someone who could hook him up with a job. How close were people in the Italian restaurant business, anyway? "You also tend bar in America?"

"Yes. I get license when I go."

"What city?"

Before he could answer, the owner came back over and asked us how our food was so far. I guess Hadrian must have forgotten what I asked, because he changed subjects once the owner was gone again.

"I say you are pretty because you are... really pretty."

If you could hear him in real life, you would understand why I was so taken aback with that relatively simple statement. Hadrian struggled to come up with the adequate words, but his brain failed him. Even when he showed me his dictionary purporting that I was beautiful, gorgeous, radiant, I still preferred the words that had come out of his mouth, because they had been with his voice. I'm sure I would have loved the words in Turkish as much, but since I couldn't understand them, nor had he said them... wait...

"Say it again, but in your home language."

His shy smile as he considered it killed me inside. When he spoke... God, the words! They were definitely Turkish. I had heard enough Turkish pop music to make those sounds out. Too bad I didn't understand any of them.

Well, I didn't understand them on the word-by-word level, but I understood the intent behind them. This man was saying that I was so beautiful that I knocked him off his feet and prevented him from speaking like a coherent, intelligent man. He had no senses around me. Instead, all he could think about was pleasing me, emotionally and physically. He wanted to lose himself in me. He wanted to stay up all night with me and discover what it meant to lock out the rest of the world and not give a single fuck about what other people thought.

I got all that from one sentence in his native language. Because when a man can speak confidently? God. Right in the heart. And the loins. If he thought I was killing him? He truly had no idea what he did to me.

After our all-American dinners, he asked me if we should go for a walk. By then it was almost seven, and if we followed the same pattern from last time, we would get coffee, walk, and *then* ahem.

Except I wanted to make sure we stayed in my neighborhood. I could already see his eyes scanning the area for a love hotel. Hold on, man, there were other things we had to do first. Put your wallet away! Not everything needed to be paid for.

We walked up and down the neighborhood, since unfortunately there were no parks in the area. There, however, a Shinto shrine that still had open grounds even though no clergy were present. We sat on a bench as the air grew colder. I worked up the nerve to ask him back to my place.

Instead, he leaned over and kissed me on the cheek. The man who didn't like impromptu touching, even from people he liked – he kissed me in public!

"What was that for?" I giggled, because that was how damn giddy I was. "I could kiss you too, you know."

"Sorry, sorry." Why was he apologizing? "I am very excited today."

"Really? About what?"

His look was more than puzzling.

"*Doushite?*" Sometimes it was easier to speak in Japanese.

"Because soon I go to America. And because I am with you tonight."

Ahhh! Flames of embarrassment on my face! The sides of them!

"Maybe I see you in America one day."

Wouldn't that be something else? I had no idea where he was going. He never asked me where I was from. We knew how futile those hopes were. With our luck, he'd be moving to Miami and I would be in Portland. Or, even worse, he would move somewhere like San Francisco or Los Angeles. So close, yet still so damn far away.

Why would we do that to ourselves? This needed to stay a fling. My vacation fling, his pre-move fling. We were in one of those indie films that make you feel like you're on the precipice of a happy ending, only to have it yanked away in the final scene. Oh, come on. Not a tragedy! More like bittersweet: the couple get on their separate planes with smiles on their faces, but never see each other again.

Hadrian smiled. Stared at his feet in the night and smiled. Whatever he was thinking about… was it about me? Was he excited to be with me again? Was he pretending, like I was, that this was the beginning of a fun relationship that could one day be something more?

I nudged him. "It's cold, huh?"

"Yes, so cold."

"Maybe we should go."

"We go?"

He could say that phrase all night as far as I was concerned. "Sure. You want to go back to my place?"

Even if he understood me, he probably didn't believe me. I was going to have to bring out the big language guns.

"*Atashi no heya ni kaerimashou ka?*"

Hadrian's eyes widened. Oh, yeah, he definitely understood me. I took him by the hand and pulled him off the bench.

"*Daijyoubu,*" I reassured him. "It's not far."

We were actually at the shrine a two minute walk away from my share house. I wasn't sure Hadrian was going to make it, though. He kept looking at me as if I asked for the impossible. Suppose I made the grand mistake of telling him that I live in a share house. Hadn't he once told me that he hates living with other people and having to listen to them?

Yeah, I knew what I was doing. My only hope was that he would play along.

My neighbors were having one of their weekly parties where they eat homecooked food and drink a fuckton of wine. I've hung out with them before, but usually my schedule conflicts with such things. And honestly, one of the reasons I went on vacation to a country that covets personal isolation is because I was tired of having to do groups multiple times a week like I do here in America.

That said, I was happy to see them. Unlike Hadrian, who did *not* like having to follow me all the way toward the kitchen to get to my room.

"Hey!" My Turkish neighbor waved at us. She approached... and stopped the moment she saw the mysteriously handsome stranger following me. "Oh, you have a guest? Nice. You can come hang out with us if you want." The others raised their wineglasses behind her.

I opened my bedroom door and ushered Hadrian inside. "Be right back," I hissed before closing the door again.

My neighbors raised their eyebrows at me.

"Your boyfriend?" asked the Turkish neighbor.

"Kinda." I lowered my voice. "Is our wonderful neighbor and his girlfriend in tonight?"

She snorted. "Yes. We were going to party very loudly, just for them. They never join us because they are so busy."

"Don't suppose y'all could hit up the karaoke place down the street for a few hours?"

"You have plans with your boyfriend?" She leaned against the wall. "Where is *he* from?"

I grinned. "Greece. But I think originally from Turkey."

"Turkey! Really? He speaks Turkish?"

"Suuuure does." If only she knew what kind of Turkish he often spoke to me.

"Wow. So you gonna have a nice night, huh?"

"Yup. Nice and loud, if you know what I mean."

She did. Her eyebrows shot up her forehead with sudden understanding. "I see. Well, maybe we can go to karaoke for a while. I think we're drunk enough to enjoy it. Of course, we won't invite our certain neighbor."

I winked at her before opening my door. "Thanks."

My door couldn't blot out the others too well, but that only allowed me to talk to Hadrian without being heard. The man stood in the middle of my narrow room with a look of perpetual confusion and hands respectfully in his pockets.

"My neighbors won't be here much longer," I assured him. "Sorry my room is small."

The voices in the hallway grew louder as people grabbed jackets and shoes before heading out the main entrance. Hadrian waited until the front door slid shut. "We are alone?"

"Oh, yeah." I took both of his hands and lured him toward my long, twin-sized bed. Perfect for forced proximity, hm? "We're as alone as we can be."

The shitty neighbors must have been asleep for them to be so quiet right now. I guessed it wouldn't stay that way for long.

\* \* \*　一期一会　\* \* \*

## Chapter 11

If Hadrian was hungry for me on our first date? He was famished now.

I take a lot of the credit. He knew how game I was. He knew what I was down for. He even knew how damn good I felt. With the awkwardness of a first time together out of the way, there was no reason for us to not go straight from first base to third. After all, I had been making myself silly thinking of this man's assets. If he needed help getting hard, I was his!

"Wow," he said with his usual fervor as I grabbed him through his jeans. "Already?"

"What? You wanna watch a movie and eat popcorn?" I nipped that goatee as if it were grown for me. "You want to make me wait? 'Cause I don't think you want to wait."

"Nooo." He flopped down against my bed. The frame shook beneath his muscular weight. "No waiting. Just surprise. You are interesting."

I laughed.

"Is it American style?"

Oh, I'm sure he would love to think all American women were like me. After all, he was moving there! "It's my style."

He pulled me down on top of him, the brute, sexual force of his action turning me on until I almost forgot we weren't *totally* alone in the share house. "I like your style," he said. "It's good."

Would it be okay if I kissed him first? It better have been. Because I was going to show that man how a real kiss worked.

It was not my first time getting dirty in a small bed. I had gone to college, after all. (No further comment on that.) I knew how to maximize the space and make the most out of a wall coming for you. For one, you could use that wall to brace the bottoms of your feet against. Especially handy when you had a strong man going fucknuts on your chest because hell yeah, you've got big tits and your man is totally bonkers for breasts.

I daresay Hadrian gave them a *lot* more attention than he did the other night when he was too desperate to get inside of me to give me the attention I truly deserved. He wasn't shy about sucking both of my nipples until they were too erect to be real. He didn't even hold back from doing at least one thing I had never done before – take a cock between them.

I wish you could have seen the smug look on his face as he fucked my cleavage. Probably a dream come true for him.

A dream that apparently ended with him coming everywhere on my chest, but I wasn't interested in that. It wasn't going to make me loud enough for my plan.

"I can think of better places for you to stick that thing."
Yeah. My pussy.

Ladies and gentlemen who may be reading this adventure, I am happy to report that Hadrian managed to bring one crucial thing along with him that night. A condom. A beautiful, glorious condom that probably actually fit him this time! I didn't even have to get the ones that I bought the other day! (Good thing, because I honestly had no idea where they were.)

"How you want?" I loved it when his voice became as deep as my need for him. His eyes glazed over. I imagined it took a shitton of concentration to get English words out of his mouth. In a perfect world, he would be talking dirty in one of his more native languages instead of one of the only ones I knew.

"Hard," I muttered. "Give it to me hard."

Hadrian didn't say anything. The man certainly didn't have to. I could see his intent in his dark eyes, the sneer of accomplishment on his lips, and the curling of his fingers as they dug into my hips and brought me closer to his.

I didn't need prompting when it came to being loud that night. I daresay he didn't either!

Everything I could've wanted transpired. The great, riveting sex that pinned me to my bed and made me feel like the most coveted, the most tantalizing woman in the world. The delicious man who had gone out of his way to see me even though he could have moved on to the next woman. The slam of my bed against the wall, of course. And Hadrian? How about the way he roared like a tiger unleashed from its cage when he came the first time, crying out in English, Japanese, some other language my brain couldn't comprehend because it was too busy processing my climax as well.

My really, really loud climax.

Most women like to say they would be way too embarrassed to know they had an audience while they had sex. Normally, I would've been the same way, although after you get busy in a college dorm room a share house isn't much different… especially when your neighbor is a fuckin' douche.

Sure enough, I had barely come down from my high when I heard grumbling on the other side of the wall. Couldn't make it out, nor could I care.

"*Wow.*" Hadrian could be as pleased with himself as he wanted while I grabbed my phone and plugged in my alarm. "I'm sleepy."

"Good. You should get some sleep." I pointed to my alarm. "'Cause we're getting up in two hours to do it again."

I think you can figure out the rest.

\*\*\*

Saying goodbye to Hadrian early the next morning was harder than I expected. This was it. This was absolutely the last time we were ever going to see each other again for the rest of our lives. One thing if this was the first and only time. Except this was the second time. We knew each other better. We had established a relationship, for better or for worse. I was already convinced that I would think of him fondly for the rest of my life. I must have been right, because here I am writing this!

Still... can you blame me for not wanting to see him go?

I think he had the same feeling, for he took his time getting dressed while the early morning light filtered through my blinds. Next door, my stupid neighbor whined to his girlfriend that he couldn't sleep. Hadrian glanced toward the wall we shared with that man and said, "He complains too much."

I laughed. "You feel pretty good about yourself, huh?"

It's a fact that your foreign language abilities go up when you get laid. Hadrian totally understood me, which he proved when he said, "I feel good with you."

Damnit. Why did he have to make this harder?

He kissed me goodbye, our lips lingering together now that he wasn't fueled with the need to consume my whole face. Good for him. I wanted to consume his face if it meant he stayed with me a little longer.

How would I meet a man like him back in America? Ugh.

"I enjoy meeting you," he said, wrapping his scarf around his neck. "Have good trip back to America."

"I should be telling you to have a safe trip." I followed him to my door. "You're the one moving there."

"Ah, we'll both have safe trips."

Hadrian spared me one last smile before showing himself out... and right into my neighbor, en route to make a big, nasty breakfast I would probably have to clean up.

"Sorry," Hadrian said. My bearded French neighbor stared wide-eyed at this guy who was shorter and leaner than him. It helped that Hadrian walked with that effortless confidence that said *I just got laid, bud.* I know enough guy speak.

"Uh… I…"

I leaned against my doorway, my sleep shorts and T-shirt so mussed from sex and sleep that I must have looked the blushing sight. "Good morning. Sleep well?"

If I had to let go of Hadrian, then it was only right I got that perturbed look of defeat from the neighbor I hated so damn much. Finally. Vengeance was mine.

# Chapter 12

Portland somehow managed to be wetter and colder than Japan when I got back one dreary Monday afternoon. My journey was so damn long and ridiculous that I think I slept for a whole week.

I attempted to get back to my usual life.

Work and the holidays gave me something to do and look forward to. Friends were happy to come by to visit and hear my crazy tales of going to bars in Japan and, you know, meeting a few people. They blushed to hear tales of my neighbor who kept me up all night, and not in the fun way. They couldn't believe it when I let slip how I got back at him.

"Do you have a picture of him?" they always asked. Luckily, Hadrian had never unmatched from my profile, so I could show off the hot man who turned my life upside down and backward in Japan. Most of my friends agreed that he was fine to look at.

Other things were on my mind as well. After all, a condom had broken when I was with Hadrian, and I had no other forms of birth control on hand. Can you blame me when I say I was a bit obsessed with that fact?

I have opened this story by proclaiming it a Romance based on some crazy real life events. We all know that most life events don't result in happily ever afters, but Romance stories demand them. Isn't that why we read them? To know that something like that is possible? To believe, even if for a moment, that our own happily ever afters are out there waiting for us? That we can meet Mr. or Mrs. Right by chance and never see life the same way again?

So I have presented this story as a romance. I fully intend on giving you quite the ending.

Yet that ending didn't come until late January, when the snow and ice began to thaw after one of the craziest storms Portland had seen in over a decade. Three of my friends approached me to go to the opening of a new restaurant everyone was talking about. Nobody could tell me what kind of food they made, and I didn't care. I may be one of the pickiest people in the world, but if others are buying, I'll go anywhere and at least pick at some plates

We hustled in our boots and most stylish jackets to the downtown center, where restaurants vie for prime real estate in a so-called foodie scene. Like I said, I'm a picky eater and nearly impossible to impress when it comes to cuisine. Can't say I'm proud of it, but those are the cards my taste buds have dealt me. I take what I can get when it comes to good food.

(I prayed that it was Italian. Guess what? I was right!)

"Oh, this is dangerous," one of my friends said as we were seated in the last available table in a crowded restaurant. "We're going to end up in a coma from the breadsticks alone."

God willing, huh? I love me a good carb coma! Is there anything better?

How about the fates conspiring to make one of your dreams come true?

Sometimes I pretended that I would see Hadrian again. That there was a chance. That the man I had a lot of things to say to would cross my path one day and we would share one of his adorable smiles. Yet I'm a realist. I understand what the odds of something like that are in this huge world...

...This huge world that isn't so huge after all.

"Hello! What would you like to..."

Our waiter – who was *very* smartly dressed for a waiter, I might add – stopped short in front of our table.

You know, if I had been in Hadrian's shoes, I probably would have thought I was seeing ghosts as well.

Whatever English he had rehearsed for his role in this restaurant, none of it was good enough for dealing with his current situation. Nor was I prepared to see the man who swept me off my swipin' right feet appear before me on my home turf.

"Hadrian?" I wasn't the only one shocked. After all, my friends had seen his picture. "Is that you?"

"I..." He put his tablet down. Someone dressed more like the waiters I expected to see approached and asked if we were all right. "It's fine, Kim," Hadrian said, his accent betraying those practiced words. "These guests are special tonight. They eat free."

Whoa! He got to make that call? He must have been high up on the food chain.

I really had no idea.

Hadrian approached me on the other side of the table. "You live in this town?"

"Uh, yeah. You moved here?"

Kim the waitress glanced between us before smiling. "I'll leave you to it, boss."

"Boss?"

"Ah…" I never thought I'd see Hadrian's goofy smile again. "This is my restaurant."

"What!"

After an assertion like that, you can bet your ass I demanded he explain some things to me. In private, no less.

He took me back to his office. His spacious, tastefully decorated office that was a mix of Mediterranean chic and preferences he picked up during his several years in Japan. Nothing was cheap. Not even close.

"I… uh…"

Hadrian grinned at me. "You are still beautiful, yes?"

Sheesh, man! Give a girl an explanation before you slather it on thick!

Hadrian had apparently not been totally forthright with me when we met back in Japan. Why would he have been, when it was only a one-night stand and nothing more? But no, he never thought to tell me that after moving to Tokyo he worked his ass off in the bar circuit, saving as much money as he could while establishing powerful connections around the world – particularly in America. This restaurant was *his*. If it did as well as he projected, he would be opening up another one on the east side… and maybe a couple in California! Hadrian was going to have an Italian restaurant empire to rival his biggest competitors.

How the fuck was I supposed to respond to that?

"Maybe it is fate." I was so enthralled with his change of clothes – gone were the jeans and leather, and hello finely tailored shirt and pants – that I almost didn't hear him speak. "We met on the other side of the world only to end up here."

That's when I dropped my purse. I'd test his definition of fate *really* quick!

"There's something I've gotta tell you." I looked around the office, paranoid that there were cameras somewhere, ready to make me feel like a total fool. "Remember how things got kinda scary on our first date?"

I hoped he understood me. As it turned out, he did.

"I…"

"How many kids you want, Mr. Rich Entrepreneur?"

When he hugged me a few minutes later, that ridiculous cologne taking me back to those fun nights together, all I could think was that we would be up all night many, many more times. Fate had decreed it, and I have long learned to not ignore fate when it sends you a busy neighbor who puts ridiculous ideas in your head.

## Up All Night

(Hadrian and I have been married a good while now, although I drew the line at his parents moving in with us. They can stay across the street, because a girl needs to write her romance tosh in private. Ahem.)

(PS: He's a much better kisser now.)

**Cynthia Dane** spends most of her time writing in the great Pacific Northwest. And when she's not writing, she's dreaming up her next big plot and meeting all sorts of new characters in her head.

She loves stories that are sexy, fun, and cut right to the chase. You can always count on explosive romances - both in and out of the bedroom - when you read a Cynthia Dane story.

Falling in love. Making love. Love in all shades and shapes and sizes. Cynthia loves it all!

### Connect with Cynthia on any of the following:

**Website:** http://www.cynthiadane.com
**Twitter:** http://twitter.com/cynthia_dane
**Facebook:** http://facebook.com/authorcynthiadane

# Up All Night

Cynthia Dane

# Up All Night

Cynthia Dane

# Up All Night

Cynthia Dane

# Up All Night

Cynthia Dane

# Up All Night

Cynthia Dane

# Up All Night

Cynthia Dane

Printed in Great Britain
by Amazon

36980567R00081